Praise for

SCARLET and IVY

"This is one of the best books I have ever read. It was exciting, funny, warm and mysterious." **Lily, aged 9**

"The whole book was brilliant… after the first paragraph it was as though Ivy was my best friend." **Ciara, aged 10**

"This book is full of excitement and adventure – a masterpiece!" **Jennifer, aged 9**

"This is a page-turning mystery adventure with puzzles that keep you guessing." **Felicity, aged 11**

"A brilliant and exciting book." **Evie, aged 8**

"The story shone with excitement, secrets and bonds of friendship… If I had to mark this book out of 10, I would give it 11!" **Sidney, aged 11**

SOPHIE CLEVERLY was born in Bath in 1989. She wrote her first story at the age of four, though it used no punctuation and was essentially one long sentence. Thankfully, things have improved somewhat since then, and she has earned a BA in Creative Writing and MA in Writing for Young People from Bath Spa University.

Now working as a full-time writer, Sophie lives with her partner in Wiltshire, where she has a house full of books and a garden full of crows.

Books by Sophie Cleverly

The Scarlet and Ivy series
in reading order

THE LOST TWIN

THE WHISPERS IN THE WALLS

THE DANCE IN THE DARK

THE LIGHTS UNDER THE LAKE

THE CURSE IN THE CANDLELIGHT

THE LAST SECRET

SCARLET
and
IVY

The Last Secret

SOPHIE CLEVERLY

HarperCollins *Children's Books*

First published in Great Britain by
HarperCollins *Children's Books* in 2019
HarperCollins *Children's Books* is a division of HarperCollins*Publishers* Ltd,
HarperCollins Publishers
1 London Bridge Street
London SE1 9GF

The HarperCollins website address is
www.harpercollins.co.uk
4

ISBN 978–0–00–821823–2

Typeset in Lido 11pt by Palimpsest Book Production Ltd, Falkirk, Stirlingshire
Printed and bound in Great Britain by CPI Group (UK) Ltd, Croydon, CR0 4YY

For all the readers of Scarlet and Ivy.
This last secret is for you...

Chapter One

IVY

The last secret was waiting for us in a drawer at the bottom of our father's desk.

But the first surprise had been Father inviting us back for the holidays. Last time we'd been home, our stepmother had told us in no uncertain terms that she didn't want us setting foot in their cottage ever again. But that chilly December, Father had telephoned our new headmistress at Rookwood School and told her that he would be picking us up instead of his sister – our Aunt Phoebe.

My twin, Scarlet, and I clambered out of Father's motor car, taking in the sight of our home as we breathed frosty plumes into the air like dragons. I was trying to remember it all in case we were forbidden from returning once more.

It was a large cottage that could have come straight from a fairy tale, all bright stone with a perfectly thatched roof. Whereas Aunt Phoebe's house was a working cottage – mud on the floors and dusty coats hung up on hooks – this place seemed to exist only to look pretty. As I gazed at it, I felt nothing but cold, inside and out. There was an iron gate that opened on to the pristine lawn where we had once sat with our suitcases, Scarlet waiting to go to Rookwood and me to Aunt Phoebe's – it seemed like a lifetime ago. The roses clambering up the stone walls could have been beautiful, tinged with white frost, but they were beginning to brown and wither, and the thorns looked sharp.

It was funny how quickly the seasons could change from one to the other. It seemed only moments ago that we'd suffered an ordeal on All Hallows' Eve, and shuffled through autumn leaves to the bonfire on Guy Fawkes Night. Now there were only two days left before Christmas, and here we were, at a place I thought we'd never see again.

Father walked up to the front door with our luggage, humming to himself. Scarlet and I followed, sharing a nervous glance as we crunched our way up the path. What were we going to find inside? I was sure our stepmother wouldn't be pleased that Father had ignored her wishes and invited us back to the house.

But as the door was unlocked and we were led inside, we found the place cold and quiet – as if no one else was there.

"Where's Edith?" Scarlet asked.

Father dropped our luggage and leant back against the door. He seemed a little out of breath. "Oh. Hmm. Probably out shopping, I expect."

That didn't quite make sense. There were no shops for miles around, and we'd been in the motor car, so how would she have got there? Unless Father had dropped her off and forgotten about it, but that seemed unlikely.

I peered into the sitting room and the kitchen, but both were empty, nothing but ashes in the fireplaces. A Christmas tree stood in a corner, with a few sad-looking baubles drooping from it and some boxes wrapped up underneath. There were stockings hanging on the mantelpiece, but from a glance I could see that there were only three, with our stepbrothers' names – Harry, Joseph and John – sewed on.

"What about the boys?" I added, half expecting them to ambush us and start throwing things. "Where are they?"

Father put his hand over his eyes. He looked a little unwell, I thought. There was a strange tinge to his skin. "Probably...

Probably playing outside. Yes." He nodded, and then wandered off, leaving us standing there in the hallway.

It was most odd. We spent the rest of the afternoon sitting in our old bedroom, wearing as many of our clothes as possible to try to keep warm.

Scarlet was doing star jumps and blowing on her hands. "Do you think there's any chance we'll get some good presents this year?"

I shook my head. "Probably socks again."

My twin looked down at her feet. "Right now," she said, "I'd be happy with an extra pair of socks."

As the evening began to draw in, we heard a crash and a stampede of footsteps downstairs that probably signalled the arrival of our stepmother and her boys. I looked up from the book I was reading and saw Scarlet's expression – she was clearly dreading our first interaction with them as much as I was.

After a while, I heard Harry shout up the stairs: "Twins! Dinner!"

Scarlet stomped out of our room. "We have names, you know!" she shouted back. Reluctantly, I put my book down and followed her downstairs. I braced myself for the impending confrontation. Surely our stepmother would throw us out as soon as she saw us?

But to my surprise, she barely acknowledged us as we

walked in. I saw her eyes narrow, but she said nothing – just handed us two plates with fairly reasonable helpings of pie and mash on them. "Go on, then," she said, waving us towards the table and turning away.

I breathed a sigh of relief. Perhaps things wouldn't be as bad as we'd thought. The fire was roaring in the kitchen, and things began to feel a little warmer.

We ate in silence, almost afraid to speak in case we broke whatever spell had caused our stepmother not to throw us out immediately. The boys nattered with their mouths open, which was enough to fill the air with noise (and, in some cases, food). Father eventually came in, and Edith jumped up to give him his plate.

"Here you go, dear," she said in the voice she only used when talking to him. "This one is yours. Thank you for dropping us off earlier."

"Oh," he said again, looking at it in a strange sort of confusion. "Yes. Thank you." He took it to the table and began to dig in.

I started to wonder if he was becoming even more absent-minded than usual, like Aunt Phoebe. It seemed to be getting worse. He hadn't remembered that he'd dropped them off anywhere – unless our stepmother was lying about that for some reason. But I filed the thought away and tried to enjoy having a half-decent meal.

We finished dinner, and the boys quickly ran away. I could hear them pulling on the Christmas tree in the next room, and rattling the presents.

Father looked up from the last of his food. "Girls," he said, and I jumped a little, not expecting the attention. "I found something I wanted to show you." He put his knife and fork down and stood up. "Come on."

We followed him, and I saw Edith frowning even harder as we left our plates behind. I had to smile a little at that. I knew from experience that she had probably been about to order us to do the washing-up.

"What do you think this is about?" Scarlet whispered to me as we headed down the hallway towards Father's office.

"No idea," I replied.

The fire inside his office had been lit too, and we felt the warmth as he held the door open for us. For a moment he stopped there, as if uncertain of what he was doing.

"Ah, yes," he said. "I was going to show you something, wasn't I?"

Scarlet looked at me, and I gave her a confused glance in return.

Father went over to his desk and sat down on the chair. "I've been thinking a lot about your mother lately," he said.

My mouth dropped open. I'm not sure I could have been

more surprised if he'd said, "I'm planning a trip to the moon."

Our mother had died when we were born, and Father never talked about it, especially not since he'd married Edith. The thought of our mother seemed to be so painful for him that he often avoided thinking about us too. And now here he was, suddenly initiating a conversation about her.

"What?" Scarlet exclaimed.

He didn't seem to notice our surprise. "I still have some things of hers, you know," he said. He wasn't even talking to us, more to the frost on the windows that was shrinking back from the heat of the fire. "I've been keeping them locked away. But after your theatre performance – after I met your aunt for the first time, and what she told me about her..."

He started coughing and then trailed off. It took me a moment to recall what he was talking about, but I realised he meant our Aunt Sara. We had tracked her down when we discovered our mother's true identity: that her maiden name had been Ida Jane Smith, not Emmeline Adel as we had been told. She had taken the name of her friend who was killed by Rookwood's former headmaster, Mr Bartholomew, in a punishment that had gone horribly wrong. When Aunt Sara had met Father, she had told him all this, or at least some of it.

Scarlet leant forward and waved a hand at him. "Yes?" she said.

He blinked at her, and then carried on. "I only locked them up because I had a lot to think about. I found myself wondering if I had ever really known her. But then I thought..." He sighed, picked up his pipe between his fingers and twirled it. "No. It's no matter. She was my Emmeline, and yours. I think perhaps I was giving the past too much weight. It was a lot to bear."

Now it was my turn to be unable to meet his eye. It just seemed so strange for Father to be speaking to us like this – or even to be speaking to us at all.

"I decided to go through her things last week," he said. "And I thought you girls should have this." He reached down and opened the bottom drawer of his desk, pulling out a gift-wrapped parcel tied with a red bow. He handed it to Scarlet, who was nearest. "Merry Christmas and all that," he said.

I nodded with wide eyes at Scarlet, and she immediately began tearing off the wrapping. Father wasn't even watching us now, just staring out of the window again.

Inside was a brown cardboard box that Scarlet pulled open. And inside the box...

Firstly, there were two photographs. Scarlet pulled them out. In one, our mother and father's faces gazed back at us.

They stood together in front of a draped wall. Our mother clad in a beautiful white lace gown and headdress, and Father in a suit with a flower in the buttonhole. They were wearing the slightly serious faces of people who had to stay still for a photograph, but their happiness shone from their eyes.

"Your wedding picture," I breathed. Why had Father never shown us this before? My glance lingered on it, taking in the details. I smiled at the sight of the familiar pearl necklace I'd inherited – a few dots of white round our mother's neck – and at the bunch of white roses in her hand. Her arm was linked with Father's. Things that perhaps meant nothing to anyone else, but meant everything to me and Scarlet.

Scarlet was smiling too. She put the photograph aside gently, taking great care not to damage it.

The one below was just as special. It was the two of them together again, but a little more recently. The picture was taken at a lake, with trees in the background. I wondered where it was, but it was nowhere I recognised – a strange reminder that our parents had had a whole life before us. This time our mother was wearing a dark-coloured cloche hat and a silky looking dress, and Father's arm was round her. The bump under her dress gave away the fact that she was clearly several months pregnant.

I felt a lump rising in my throat.

Beneath the pictures, there was a fairly large carved wooden box, shiny with polish. Scarlet lifted it out and held it up to the light. Tiny silhouettes of ballerinas danced round the outside. Hesitantly, she lifted the catch on the front.

A familiar tune began to play, and a tiny ballerina in a white dress popped up from inside the box. She spun around in a never-ending pirouette, dancing in the firelight. Occasionally the tinny music gave a little jolt, and she would tilt slightly before carrying on.

We peered inside. There were a few trinkets in the bottom – some old rings and a pressed white rose that I realised was probably left over from their wedding.

Scarlet put the box down on the desk and threw her arms round Father, who looked shocked. "Thank you!" she exclaimed. "This is the best present ever!"

When she let go, he smiled softly for a moment. "Don't mention it," he said. Then his eyes slipped over us, and he went back to staring out of the window again. The moment melted away like the frost.

Chapter Two

SCARLET

For the next few days, I couldn't stop thinking about the present we'd been given. Even on Christmas Day, when we didn't receive a single gift, it almost didn't matter. Father had given us something more special than anything you could buy at a fancy department store. He'd given us a piece of the puzzle that was our mother.

I'd barely noticed our stepmother's stern looks over Christmas lunch. I hadn't corrected Father when he accidentally called me "Ivy" twice. I hadn't even had the urge to punch Joseph and John when they tried to put carrots in my hair.

I looked at the box and the photographs every chance I got. I almost felt like our mother was going to step out of them, somehow. Ivy and I opened the music box over and over again, watching the ballerina spin until the clockwork ran down and the final notes chimed slowly into the air.

"I know this tune," Ivy had said after the first few listens. "It's from the ballet *Swan Lake*!" I knew she was right as soon as she said it. I had sometimes heard our ballet teacher, Miss Finch, playing it on her piano.

But the more we listened, the more something began to stand out to me. It was that tiny jolt in the music. I held my ear close to it, and could hear a little click each time.

That Christmas evening, sitting on the floor in our dusty old bedroom, I opened it up again. I wondered if it always happened, or only sometimes. Was it just an accident, something that had been put together wrongly in the clockwork? Was I even hearing what I thought I could hear?

"Do you hear it too?" I asked Ivy, who was peering down at me from her bed.

"The funny click?" she said.

I nodded and flipped the lid shut once more. "What do you think it is?"

She wrinkled her nose. "Perhaps it's a bit broken?"

It was possible, I supposed. I picked it up and gently turned it over, hearing the rings inside tumble up into the lid. There wasn't any damage to it that I could see – in fact it looked pristine.

Ivy slipped off her bed and sat on the floor next to me. "Wait," she said, after staring at the box for a few moments. "Open it again."

I did as she said, and she pointed into it as the tune played. "Look. The inside isn't as deep as the outside..."

Peering more closely, I saw that she was right. There was at least an inch or so on the bottom below where the rings and the pressed rose sat.

"I don't know," Ivy continued. "Perhaps it's just where the mechanism goes."

I shook my head. "No," I said. "I've seen one of these opened up before. All of the mechanics are under the ballerina." I pointed to the miniature wooden stage that she was attached to. "But there could be something else under here." I began running my fingers round the edges, and sure enough, I thought I could feel a seam in the wood. "Hmm."

That was when the idea struck me.

As the ballerina wound down, I folded her away and then opened the box again. But this time, when I heard the strange click in the tune, I pressed on the side as hard as I could.

And much to our surprise, a drawer shot out of the bottom of the box.

"Gosh!" Ivy exclaimed, nearly falling sideways.

We both stared into the secret drawer. Inside it was a sheaf of folded paper, a little yellowed but mostly untouched by time.

"Please tell me it's not diary pages," Ivy said. "I don't want to find any more..."

I poked her indignantly. Those diary pages I'd left her to find had saved me from a horrible fate in an asylum after our evil headmistress sent me there, thank you very much.

I pulled the papers out and flattened them on the floor. There were several, and they were covered in writing – or, more specifically, in numbers.

"Oh," said Ivy as she pored over them. "Isn't this—"

"The Whispers' code!" I interrupted her.

It was a long story, but we'd discovered last year that our mother had attended Rookwood School, just like we did. And during that time, she'd been in a secret club whose members called themselves the Whispers in the Walls, fighting back against the nasty Mr Bartholomew. We'd found their coded book of accusations against him, and our best friend Ariadne had been able to translate it.

"We'll have to take this to Ariadne," Ivy said, and I nodded. If it was the same code, she would be able to tell us what it said.

But there was something else. As I leafed through the pages, I saw that there was something written on the back of the last one. I turned it over. It was real writing, not just numbers. The top line read:

For my husband

Ivy and I looked at each other in shock. Could this be a letter from our mother? Her last secret? We read on.

I hope that I am with you now, safe and well, and able to tell this all to you in person. If I am not, then I pray it is not because he has found me. I shouldn't have got involved again. I see that now. If you can interpret the secrets I have written on these pages, then perhaps you will be able to act where I could not. But I beg you, proceed with the utmost caution. It is a path fraught with danger and corruption.

I wanted to tell the truth, but if I

never do, just know this: I am sorry for what I have hidden. Everything I did has been with the best of intentions. I wanted to expose everything that he has done, to free the past and change the future for the better. Perhaps it is too late for that now.

My name is Ida Jane Grey. I love you.

My hands were shaking so much that I almost dropped the paper. Our mother was speaking to us from the past, like a ghost.

"*I pray it is not because he has found me,*" Ivy whispered. "Who's *he*? Mr Bartholomew?"

"It must be," I said, although I had no way to be sure, since we couldn't read the coded writing. But our mother had spent her life running from him, so it seemed to make sense.

Ivy put her hand over her mouth. "You don't think... he did something to her?"

I thought about it for a moment, but then I shook my head with certainty. "Our mother died in childbirth, didn't she? I don't see how the headmaster could have had anything to do with that. And whatever this says..." I turned the pages over in my hands, "...nobody's got their hands on it for years. I don't think Father had any idea these were in here."

"We're the first to see these since she hid them," Ivy said, staring down in awe. I handed them to her and watched as she ran her fingers over the words.

"I need to know what it says!" I declared, jumping up. I wished we were seeing Ariadne sooner, but there was still over a week to go before we were due back at school. How was I supposed to bear having to wait that long? "It could be more information about the Whispers, more accusations!"

"Well..." Ivy replied hesitantly. "It might all be meaningless now. We got Mr Bartholomew thrown in jail. We exposed what he did to our mother's friend. What else could there be?"

I sank back down on the bed, the spark from the new secret beginning to fizzle out. "Hmmph. You're probably right."

But I still felt a tingle in my fingertips from where I'd held the pages. Whatever was written there, whether it was important now or not – it had been important to our mother when she wrote it. That was what mattered. We'd never known her, but now we had something she'd left behind, that only we had seen. It was something special that could never be taken away.

Chapter Three

IVY

The holidays weren't particularly filled with cheer, but they managed to pass without any conflict, which seemed like a Christmas miracle in itself. Our stepmother was constantly glaring at us, but she mostly kept her distance.

Father, on the other hand, seemed to be getting stranger by the day. He spent most of his time in his office, and then sometimes wandered around the house with no apparent purpose. He looked a little off-colour too, and wasn't eating very much. But he seemed happy enough, in his own way. I wondered if he was still thinking about Mother.

We didn't show him the papers that we'd found – Scarlet wasn't sure if we could trust him, and we definitely didn't want to leave them anywhere Edith might come across them. I just wanted to find out what they said first.

When the New Year arrived and the day finally came for us to go back to Rookwood School, we were practically buzzing with excitement. It seemed so strange to feel that way, given how horrible the school had been for us most of the time. But now it was full of friends, noise and chatter. It was alive, while our home just felt chilly and dead.

Our stepmother was standing in our bedroom doorway that morning, with her arms folded, watching us pack. "Don't come back this time," she sneered, before marching off. Scarlet made a rude gesture after her.

While Father drove us to school, I spent the whole journey through the winding lanes thinking of the music box tucked away in my bag. We'd hidden the papers inside it again, along with the photographs. Part of me was afraid that the secret catch would stop working and they'd be trapped in the box forever, but we'd tried it several times just to make sure. Each time it sprang open like it had before.

At one point, Father started coughing so hard he had to stop the car in the middle of the road.

"Are you all right?" I asked.

It took him a few minutes before he said anything again. He'd gone rather green. "I'm fine," he said. "Just feeling a little under the weather, that's all." He slapped his face gently with his hands, recomposing himself. "Right. We must get going. I've got work to do." And off we went again.

We pulled into Rookwood, through those grand gates, the stone rooks staring down at us from their pillars. It was a January morning and there was still a layer of frost over everything, making it sparkle in the sunlight. The bare trees waved their cold limbs at us as we passed.

As we went down the drive, the familiar sight of numerous motor cars and buses greeted us – each one spilling passengers out at the front of the school. I took a deep breath. We were back.

When we finally made it to the main entrance, Father stopped the car and helped us out with our bags. He seemed to be struggling somewhat. "Here you go, girls," he said. "I hope you have a good term."

"Thank you," I said, unsure what else to say.

"I'm... sure we will," said Scarlet. She wasn't used to being on speaking terms with our father either.

Inside Rookwood's huge doors, the new headmistress, Mrs Knight, was calling instructions to the girls who were streaming in. "Straight to your dorms, please! Assembly in one hour!"

We heaved our bags upstairs through the crowd. It took some time, but we eventually made it to our assigned dorm, room thirteen.

"Let's dump our things here and then go and find Ariadne," Scarlet suggested.

"Good plan," I replied. I put my bag down in front of the wardrobe while Scarlet threw hers on her bed. Of course, there was something important I had to do first. I reached in with care and pulled out the music box, setting it down gently on the desk. It chimed quietly as it touched the wood. I hoped that it looked enough like any other trinket box that no one would think anything of it.

"I wonder who Ariadne will be sharing with?" Scarlet asked as she made a vague attempt at hanging up the few clothes she owned. A dress slid off its hanger, but she ignored it.

"Hmm." I wrinkled my nose. "No idea." Our best friend had been sharing with a girl named Muriel Witherspoon last term, but Muriel had been expelled after being responsible for a string of awful events. Now Ariadne was once again left without a roommate.

My excitement began to build at the thought of seeing Ariadne again. I'd missed her so much the past few weeks.

She always knew how to cheer us up, like a ray of sunshine through the dark brooding clouds of Rookwood.

We made our way to her dorm room, where I was pleased to see the door already flung open and our best friend beside the bed with her suitcases.

"Ariadne!" Scarlet called out, running in to hug her.

I followed and joined in.

"Hello!" Ariadne said brightly, once we'd released her from the hug. "Did you have a good Christmas?"

I shared a look with my twin. "It was... fine," I said. My thoughts immediately flashed to the music box, but we were interrupted by a voice from the doorway.

"Good morning," came a voice with a Scottish accent. If Ariadne was a ray of sunshine, this voice was rain on the moors.

"Oh," Ariadne said.

We turned round. It was the new girl, Ebony McCloud. She'd been involved in the havoc with Muriel last term, pretending to be a witch and frightening everyone. But she'd since apologised, and I supposed that at least she seemed to be trying to make up for what she'd done.

"Don't worry," she said, traipsing in with her black bag and dropping it on the opposite bed. She must have seen the look on our faces. "I won't turn you into frogs in your sleep."

Ariadne cleared her throat. "I must be forgetting my manners," she said. "Good morning, Ebony. Nice to see you again." She elbowed both of us.

"Morning," I said as brightly as I could.

"Hullo," said Scarlet.

A smile twitched at the corner of Ebony's lips. "Mrs Knight was pretty cross when she found out I was pretending to be sharing a room last term. We're always meant to share, so apparently I ruined the whole system." She sighed. "And since you're missing a roommate, Ariadne, I've been told I have to stay here."

Ariadne looked a little unsure, but she still made an effort. "Oh goody," she said.

"It's all right, honestly," Ebony said. "I won't be pulling any of those tricks from last term. I promise. I'm just Ebony now. I didn't even bring my cat." That made us smile. Her cat, Midnight, had followed her to school last term and we'd all been convinced it was her magical familiar. Maybe Ebony really had abandoned her witchy ways.

Once we were all unpacked, it was time to go to assembly. We trudged downstairs to the hall, where we all filed in. The air was filled with chatter.

Mrs Knight took to the stage. "All right, girls, settle down!"

The chatter faded to a quiet mumble before it melted away completely.

"Welcome back for the spring term, everyone." She cleared her throat. "I know we have had... difficulties in the past. But I am confident that we can push forward and make Rookwood School the best it can be!"

"Isn't this what she said last term?" Scarlet whispered, but I shushed her.

"If we all work together," Mrs Knight continued, "We can—"

She was interrupted by the doors at the back of the hall opening.

We all turned round. A man had walked in. He was fairly young, possibly in his twenties, though I couldn't guess his precise age. He had dark hair, short on the sides and slicked back on the top. He had matching dark eyes and a close-cropped beard, and he was wearing a suit that looked tailored and expensive. He proceeded to lean against the back wall with an interested expression on his face.

"We can..." Mrs Knight tried again, but then faltered, seeming unable to ignore the distraction any longer. "Excuse me, sir!" she called towards the back of the hall. "We're in the middle of assembly. Would you mind waiting outside?"

The young man looked around as if there might be

someone else she was addressing. "Oh, don't mind me, madam," he said. "I'm just observing."

There was utter silence as everyone stared at him. Few men ever set foot in Rookwood School, let alone young and well-groomed ones. And that wasn't all – there was something strangely familiar about him.

"I..." Mrs Knight was speechless for a moment. "Look, I really must insist..."

The man sighed, stepped forward and then began striding towards the front. Hundreds of eyes followed him.

"Well, if you *really must*," he said, with an unusual air of confidence. He hopped up on to the stage and stood looking out at all of us. "My name is Henry Bartholomew, son of Edgar Bartholomew, and I'm the new owner of your school."

Chapter Four

SCARLET

What? The whole school seemed to gasp at the same time.

I couldn't believe it. Of all the sentences to have come out of a stranger's mouth on the assembly-hall stage... Well, I hadn't been expecting that. He was the son of our evil former headmaster? And he *owned the school*? Why?

"We will have to talk about this elsewhere, Master Bartholomew," Mrs Knight said firmly.

He smiled back at her as if this was the most normal thing in the world. "Of course," he said, putting his hands in his pockets. "That's what I was hoping. I've got a lot of plans I want to explain to you. Oh, and do call me Barty, everyone does."

He gave a winning smile as he stepped down off the stage and to the side of the room, though I don't think anyone's gaze left him. He leant against the wall again, putting his foot up on it like he owned the place – which, according to him, he did.

Mrs Knight looked around helplessly. Her eyes rested on Miss Bowler, our loud-mouthed games teacher, who was at the side of the room. "Ah!" she said, seeming relieved that she'd found a lifeline. "Miss Bowler, while I'm dealing with this, can you come up and give the announcements for the new term?"

Miss Bowler, who always liked the chance to shout at people, bounded up on to the stage and took Mrs Knight's notes from her. "Right, then!" she boomed as the headmistress scurried off towards Henry Bartholomew. Her voice echoed from the walls. "Listen up! Hockey club will be starting next Thursday afternoon and..."

For possibly the first time ever, I don't think anyone was listening to Miss Bowler (and she was pretty difficult to ignore). We were all trying to lip-read Mrs Knight's quiet conversation with the young man in the corner. After a few minutes she led him back out of the hall, and once again all our heads turned round to follow them.

"Eyes front!" Miss Bowler yelled, and everyone snapped to attention again.

"What *is* going on?" I whispered to Ivy, once Miss Bowler was back in full flow. "And where did he come from?"

My twin just shrugged, but she looked worried. Whatever was going on... it didn't seem good.

All anyone was talking about as we left the hall was the sudden appearance of Henry Bartholomew, or *Barty* (shudder) and what it all meant.

"I can't believe Mr Bartholomew's son is here," I said. "What is he up to? Do you think he's as bad as his father?"

"I don't have any idea what you're on about," said Ebony, who was walking beside us.

Oops. This was probably going to take some explaining.

"The old headmaster," I began. "He was awful. Super strict. One of his punishments went too far and *killed* someone. We had to get him to admit it, so that the police would arrest him."

Ebony recoiled. "Oh!" she said, looking horrified.

Then I remembered something. "Ivy! We nearly forgot! We have to show Ariadne..." I trailed off, seeing Ebony's face.

After all that she'd done, had she earned enough trust to be part of our group? "Show me what?" Ariadne asked.

I looked at Ivy, but she was staring down at her timetable

and not being at all helpful. I sighed. Maybe Ebony was involved already.

"We found some papers that belonged to our mother," I explained reluctantly. "But they were in code."

Ariadne gasped. "The Whispers' code?"

"We think so," said Ivy, who was paying attention again now. "Well, we *hope* so. Otherwise it's going to take even longer to figure out what it says."

"Oh gosh," our friend exclaimed. "I'll look at it after class. How exciting!"

But as we got nearer to the Latin classroom, there was a commotion coming from within that got louder and louder. We found our Latin teacher, Miss Simons, trying to calm everyone down.

"Please!" she was begging them. "Please sit down! We must have silence!"

But no one was listening.

"What happened to Mr Bartholomew?"

"And how come his son owns the school?"

"What do you think he's going to do? Perhaps he'll fix the heating!"

I saw that even Rose, who was usually silent, was whispering excitedly to her newly returned best friend (and my former worst enemy) Violet. I waved at them, but they were too engrossed in their conversation to notice.

Miss Simons looked over at us in exasperation. "Girls, please..."

I slammed my fist down on the desk. "Everyone shut up!"

That got their attention. They all went quiet.

The Latin teacher didn't look as pleased as I'd hoped. "Scarlet," she said with a sigh, "I appreciate the effort, but that was a bit much."

"Sorry, Miss," I said. "It worked, though."

We found our seats, while Miss Simons started writing on the board. "Thank you, girls," she said. "I'm sure we'll find out about this Henry Bartholomew fellow in due course. Now, if we could please all focus on our Latin..."

The last lesson of the day for us was ballet. We ran to our room to change. I laid my hand on the music box. "Soon your secrets will be revealed," I whispered to it. Ivy rolled her eyes at me.

Our ballet lessons were held down in the school's chilly basement, with our two teachers, Miss Finch and Madame Zelda. We were the first to arrive, thanks to our speedy changing, and we stopped at the bottom of the stairs when we saw that Mrs Knight was down there talking to them.

"He says his father has died – though he didn't seem too upset about that," she said, running a hand through her greying hair.

I stepped into the room. "What? Mr Bartholomew is *dead*?"

The teachers turned to look at me.

"Oh, hello, Scarlet," Mrs Knight said. "Yes, it would appear so. I saw the death certificate. That is how this young Master Henry has come into possession of Rookwood."

Ivy looked shell-shocked. It was a bit of a surprise. Well, our former headmaster was a cruel man, and one who was very old and incredibly sickly. But it still seemed strange that he could really be dead and gone. After everything he'd done... And now his son was taking over?

"Um, anyway, yes, he tells me that he's got *plans* for the school," Mrs Knight continued. "But I'm telling everyone not to panic. I'm sure this will all be sorted out. I've arranged to meet him again at three o'clock."

"Right," said Miss Finch, sharing a worried glance with Madame Zelda. "We'll see you in the staff room."

Mrs Knight left, wringing her hands. She didn't seem as confident as her words suggested.

"This sounds fishy," I whispered to Ivy, who nodded, still wide-eyed and a little pale from the news. I wondered what these "plans" would be.

"Come on, then, girls," Miss Finch called from her seat at the piano. "Let's get warmed up."

It was always a relief to get back to dancing again. For

an hour, in front of the endless reflections in the mirrors, I could forget about everything. I didn't have to think about the secret box or our stepmother or Mr Bartholomew and his son. It was nothing but muscles and movement and music. And for once, everyone else was focused as well. Even Penny withheld her usual snide comments.

But when the lesson ended, and we'd curtseyed to the teachers, reality came rushing back.

I kept wondering exactly what Henry Bartholomew had planned for us. "Should we spy on their meeting?" I whispered to Ivy as we took off our toe shoes.

She made a face. "How would we do that? We can't just walk into the staff room – there'll be teachers in there."

Hmm. That was true. And even if we looked in through the windows, we wouldn't be able to see anything unless we were pressed up against them, and that would certainly give us away. I sighed. "I suppose we'll just have to wait and see."

At least we had something to focus on: showing Ariadne what we'd found at home. We raced back to the dorm. We still had a few hours before dinner, and Ariadne came straight to our room as soon as she'd finished with hockey. Ebony had somehow managed to get away with avoiding games all together, and was presumably still holed up somewhere writing essays on sporting activities – the task she'd been given after refusing to do sports last term.

After the news of Mr Bartholomew's death had been thoroughly dissected, we sat around on the floor of our bedroom with the music box in front of us. "So look," I said, eager to show our friend what we'd found. "You open it up and it starts to play the tune. But when you hear that strange click, you can open the secret compartment." I pulled it and there, sure enough, were the photographs and the paper covered in code.

"Oh gosh," said Ariadne as I gently handed her the papers. "How amazing! I can't believe this secret was just hiding in there for all these years!"

"Does it look like the same code you translated before?" Ivy asked anxiously.

Ariadne frowned. "I think so. Or maybe a slight variation. I'll see what I can do."

I grinned at her. "You're the best, Ariadne."

She grinned back at me. "I'm so glad to be part of the team again."

I wrapped my arm round her shoulder. "No matter what happens, you're always part of the team!" I took a deep breath. "But... perhaps don't show it to Ebony. Not just yet, anyway."

Ariadne seemed a bit perturbed about that, but nothing could ruin my excitement at that moment. We were finally going to uncover our mother's last secrets.

Chapter Five

IVY

As it turned out, we would learn about Henry Bartholomew's plans for the school sooner rather than later.

It was dinner time that same evening, and we were all filing in as usual. Well, perhaps "filing" wasn't the right word. The actual process was messier and involved a lot more shoving and name-calling.

We were in the queue for food when Scarlet started elbowing me.

"Ouch!" I exclaimed. "What is it?"

She pointed to the doorway. "Look!"

The man himself had just walked into the room. There was a noticeable drop in volume as more and more people noticed his presence. He didn't seem to be paying anyone else any attention, though. He started pacing around the dining hall, staring at the walls and the ceiling. He kept his hands in his pockets while his dark eyes searched the place... for what?

"What is he doing?" Scarlet hissed.

I had no answer.

We were so busy staring at him that we didn't notice the queue had moved on.

"Ahem!" The cook cleared her throat. "Move up, we haven't got all day!"

"Sorry," I mumbled, running to her and holding my tray out to receive the day's usual helping of stew.

By the time we'd got to our house table, Henry had made it the whole way round and headed back out of the door. What was he up to? His expression wasn't giving anything away. He just smiled confidently at the teachers on his way out.

Mrs Knight, however, was not so subtle. She was muttering something to Miss Bowler near the entrance, when Nadia walked past them.

"What do you mean you might have to *close the school*?"

Miss Bowler exclaimed, so loudly that most people heard her. And those who didn't soon knew what she'd said because the words had rippled outwards like a stone that had been dropped in a pond.

"*What?*" Scarlet said.

"*Why?*" Ariadne exclaimed.

And suddenly everyone was calling out, while Mrs Knight just stood there, the colour draining from her face.

"Girls!" she shouted, trying to stop the flow of conversation. "Girls! I need your attention, please!"

For once, people listened. I think we all wanted to know how she was going to explain this.

"Please, don't panic," she began. This wasn't entirely reassuring coming from Mrs Knight, who had been known to downplay even the worst of disasters. She cleared her throat. "As you have all heard, the school has a new owner. Mr... Henry Bartholomew has made his plans clear to us. He wants to..." She froze then, staring into the distance as if she was an actor who couldn't read the script.

"Where is she going with this?" Scarlet whispered, but I shushed her.

Mrs Knight took a deep breath and tried again. "He wants to close the building."

The noise broke out again as everyone tried to talk at the same time.

"But *why*?"

"What would happen to all of us?"

"Where would we go to school?"

"Enough!" Miss Bowler boomed, and I could have sworn the chairs rattled beneath us.

I couldn't help but notice that Mrs Knight's hands were shaking. "Everybody calm down, *please*. There has been talk of safety inspections. It may only be temporary. Nothing is set in stone. Let's just wait and see, shall we?"

With a meaningful glance at Miss Bowler, she left the room.

Miss Bowler turned to all of us. "What are you lot looking at? Spoons back in mouths and stop gaping! You will eat in silence!" Her face was red as she strode out after the headmistress.

The silence, as you can imagine, didn't last long.

"Is she being serious?" Scarlet asked, leaning over the table.

"Obviously," I replied. I was struggling to know what to say. "But maybe it's nothing. Just some inspections, like she said."

"But does he really have the power to shut the school, just like that?" my twin replied. "And if he does... couldn't he just decide to close it down permanently?"

"This is horrible," Ariadne said. Her face crumpled for

a moment, and she looked like she was about to cry, but then recovered herself. "If the school closes... we'll all be split up! Where will we go? What if I get sent back to Hightower Academy? If they'd even have me back, after I was expelled."

"We won't let that happen," said Scarlet. I raised an eyebrow at her. I didn't know how she could promise such things.

I stared down at my plate for a moment, trying to gather my thoughts. "I think we have to listen to Mrs Knight. We can't start panicking when we don't even know what Henry Bartholomew is going to decide."

Ariadne made a sort of strangled sound in frustration, and dropped her head into her hands.

I bit my lip. I wasn't sure how to feel. Rookwood had changed and it meant something different to me. Now it seemed that someone might have the power to take our school away. Not just to ruin its reputation as our old headmistress, Miss Fox, had once tried to do in a wild act of revenge, but perhaps to get rid of it all together. There would be no more secrets for us to find if it was closed down. Nothing left of our mother's legacy. No more adventures with Ariadne and Rose and the others.

What if we were sent somewhere *worse*? Or – and it didn't bear thinking about – sent back to our stepmother?

She had more or less threatened in the past that she would have us both locked up rather than live with her again.

"Let's not all start worrying about this right now," Scarlet said, unusually being the voice of reason. "Maybe we should just listen to Mrs Knight. We have bigger things to think about."

"Bigger things than the school being closed?" Ariadne asked, open-mouthed.

Scarlet poked her with a fork. "Yes, like translating that code! We have to find out what our mother was up to when she wrote that note. It could be important."

My twin was right. There was nothing we could do about Henry and his plans right now, but we could find out what was in those letters.

Ariadne puffed the air from her cheeks. "All right, of course. I'll try this evening. But how am I going to hide it from Ebony?"

"Just tell her you're doing extra arithmetic work," Scarlet told her. "Nobody would care about that."

"But I *do* have extra arithmetic wo—" Ariadne started, before wisely cutting herself off.

I lay in bed that night with my mind racing. I didn't want to think any more about what would happen to us if the school really were to shut down, so instead I tried to chase the thoughts of our mother. Just when I'd imagined there was nothing left for us to learn about her, we were on the brink of discovering more.

I silently prayed that Ariadne would be able to solve the code, that it wouldn't be something completely different that she had never encountered before. But it would make sense for our mother to use the same code that the Whispers in the Walls had used, wouldn't it? Would it reveal more secrets from her time with them?

I couldn't sleep. I needed to know.

Sitting up, I whispered to my twin, "Are you awake?"

"Ugh. Yes," she replied.

"I can't even shut my eyes," I told her. "I can't wait to find out what the papers say."

"Same," my twin said.

But then there was a knock at the door.

It was well after lights-out. That meant the person at the door was either Matron checking on us, or...

We threw the covers off, jumped up and ran to the door.

"Ariadne!" I exclaimed as I opened it.

She was standing there in her nightgown, with a jumper on top, holding the sheaf of papers. "I translated it," she whispered. I couldn't read her expression in the darkness. "All of it. I think you're going to want to know what it says."

Chapter Six

SCARLET

We ushered Ariadne inside and shut the door as quietly as we could. I went to turn the light on, but Ivy stopped me.

"Don't!" she cautioned. "If Matron gets up, she'll see it."

I didn't think this was likely, given how Matron usually slept like the dead, and it seemed incredibly late, but I supposed she was right. We shouldn't risk it.

"Don't worry," Ariadne said. "I brought a candle." She sat down on the floor and pulled out a small holder from her pocket, complete with a tealight. Then a match appeared in her other hand, and she struck it, the bright flame flaring against the wick.

"Where do you keep all this stuff?" I asked her.

"In my suitcases," she replied. That made sense. She did have far too many suitcases. "I've been decoding it non-stop since dinner. It took *hours*." She shivered. "I had to tell Ebony I was doing extra-difficult arithmetic for fun."

We sat down beside her on the patchy carpet, huddling together for warmth. She laid out the pages and her translations.

I peered at them in the flickering glow. "So it *was* the old code?"

"Yes, thank goodness. That made it easier, but still time-consuming." She pointed at what she'd written. "Start here." I began to read it aloud, as quietly as I could.

/

We moved into the cottage today. I never thought that I would be back living so close to Rookwood School. Mortimer has no idea that this is where everything began. He doesn't even know who I really am. Knowing that Rookwood is just a few squares away on the map... that he may still be there... it brings it all back into focus once more. I thought I could forget, but I cannot. The truth is there and it scares me. After all these years, I remember our old secret code. I think I have to write this down.

2

Things are clearer today. I spent all night torturing myself. I have been running from my past, hiding from it, for too long. It isn't just my truth that has been covered. My darling Emmie was killed and for all I know her killer is still right there in Rookwood School, facing no consequences. Perhaps I have been thinking about this all wrong. Moving here may be my chance to set her free.

3

I went back to Rookwood village. I persuaded my husband, Mortimer, to take me, told him it would be nice for a visit. I wore gloves in a vain attempt to hide the fact that my hands were shaking. I left him talking to the priest in the churchyard and headed to the shop. I covered my face with my scarf, praying that they wouldn't recognise me, but nobody seemed to. Speaking to some of the villagers, my worst fear was confirmed. He is indeed still running the school. The lady I spoke to first glanced all around as if he were about to jump at us from the shadows. They are almost as afraid as I am, though they seem not to know why. But they told me the rumours—

Ariadne had stopped there. I glanced up at her. "What happened?"

"She cut herself off," Ariadne said, handing me another page. Ivy leant over to see it too. "Here you go."

4

I am back. Mortimer interrupted my writing yesterday. Perhaps he cannot read *this code, but I still do not want to take any chances. He would only ask me what I am working on. I hope to tell him the truth someday, but not today.*

The rumours I was told concerned the headmaster (I do not wish to write his name). He continues to have a fearsome reputation. But they also say that he does not truly own the school, that he took it on false grounds! This is important. I must investigate further.

I looked up at the others. "Are you hearing this? Mr Bartholomew might not have been the real owner of the school! Which would mean that Henry wouldn't have inherited it. This could change everything!" I felt amazed that we'd found a secret about Mr Bartholomew so soon after his death. It was just what we needed – almost as if our mother had known, somehow.

Ariadne nodded. "Keep reading," she said.

5

I think the rumours might be true. I have done all the research I can. Rookwood was owned by an old family for centuries - how did it pass to him? One minute he was merely the headmaster; the next, I read in the newspaper that the place has always belonged to him. Something is very wrong here. I fear that the only evidence may be inside Rookwood.

6

I have made a grave mistake. I should never have gone back to that school.

Ivy gasped.

I paused and raised my eyebrows.

"She came back here?" my twin exclaimed. "I never thought..." She trailed off, speechless.

Mortimer agreed to take me there again. He thinks I have a strange fascination, but he didn't argue. This time I left him at the Fox and Hounds with his friend while I went to the school. Walking down that long driveway brought back years of memories I had tried to forget. I told the secretary that I was a prospective parent and she let me look around. Every step along the corridor felt dangerous, but I had to search for evidence. I made it to the library and I found some documents on the history of the building. But that was all. I searched other places, even the secret places I had known long ago, trying to look like an interested parent whenever anyone set eyes on me. But there was nothing.

As I went to leave, I saw him - the headmaster, Mr Bartholomew. He was striding down the hallway towards me. He met my eye for a split second, and my blood turned to frost. I quickly faced away and ducked into a nearby classroom. I still do not know if he saw me, and if he did... whether he knew I was the girl that had challenged him all those years ago. The one witness to Emmie's murder.

I am afraid, though, that he does know. I am afraid that he will find out who I am and where I live. How could I have *been so foolish? This is not for me to solve, not now that I am happy and safe and married. If I am to defeat him, I cannot be reckless. I need to be stronger. I need a plan.*

That was all she had written. There were no more pages of Ariadne's translation. I frowned. "She had all of this, and she never managed to take Mr Bartholomew down?"

"But we did," Ivy said.

I looked up at my twin. She wasn't meeting my eye, but I could see a tear glistening on her cheek. I knew how she felt. We'd been the ones who'd got justice for our mother and her friend. We'd finally stopped him.

If only she could have known back then that she'd finally be vindicated. I hated the thought that she'd died without finishing what she'd started, feeling that she'd failed. I curled my fist tightly round the pages.

"This is important," Ariadne said. "Perhaps your mother was on to something. If Mr Bartholomew didn't really own the school, then who did it belong to? Could it have been this family that she talked of?"

"Hmm." I sniffed. I was trying to pretend I wasn't on the verge of tears.

Ariadne's eyes glittered in the light. She pulled out the

remaining pages – they must have been the documents that our mother had found. They were a little yellow, folded very small and covered with curly handwriting that looked many years old. "I read these as well. It wasn't easy."

I squinted at them. Even some of the spellings looked unfamiliar, but I could make out the word *Rookwood*. "Anything useful?"

"It talks about the Lord and Lady of Rookwood. It's a bit of their family history and the history of the house, how it was originally built in the sixteen hundreds and expanded and changed over the years. It's all rather fascinating—"

"Summarise?" I said impatiently. Ivy rolled her eyes at me.

"Well," Ariadne said, "I *think* what your mother was trying to get across was that this same family, the Woottons, owned the house for many generations. It was always passed down to the eldest child or, if there wasn't one, to a cousin. It was supposed to stay in the family. So how did it end up in the hands of Mr Bartholomew?"

"Perhaps there was no one else left," Ivy suggested, running her fingertips over the paper. "And he was given it because he wanted to run the school."

"It sounds like that's what Mr Bartholomew wanted everyone to think," I said. "But what's the truth?"

Ivy smiled sadly. "It's been so long. I don't know if we'll

be able to find out." Ariadne gave a silent nod in response.

I stared into the candle flame for a moment, and I felt a flicker inside myself too. A spark of *something*. Something that would never go out.

"No, come on," I said, looking back and forth between my twin and our best friend. "This is *us* we're talking about. If there's one thing we're good at, it's finding the truth."

"But after all these years—" Ariadne started.

"We've done it before and we'll do it again. The Whispers. Miss Fox. Rose's family. We've uncovered all their secrets, haven't we?" I told them. A grin spread across my face. "The truth can't hide forever."

Chapter Seven

IVY

We were rudely awoken that morning by the sound of a commotion from the corridor. I yawned as I pulled the door open to peer out.

There was a man standing several doors down, and he appeared to be having some sort of confrontation with Matron.

"Never heard anything so ridiculous in my life!" she was shouting, waving her arms about. She still had her dressing gown on and hair rollers in. "These are *girls' dormitories*!"

There were other heads peering out of doors too. Everyone wanted to know what was going on.

"I appreciate that, madam," the man said. He was short, with silver hair and spectacles, and he was carrying a clipboard. "But I've been employed to do a full inspection of the building."

Matron shook her head in disbelief. "I don't care what you've been employed to do! I'm not letting you walk around these rooms, certainly not while they're occupied. And preferably not at all! What gives you the right?"

The man didn't seem to be particularly concerned by Matron's outburst. He looked slowly from his clipboard to his watch, not meeting her eye. "I'm sorry," he said. "But I have my orders from the owner."

Scarlet leant round me. "He doesn't sound particularly sorry," she whispered.

She was right. He didn't.

"You can't be serious," Matron said, flapping her arms. "When the headmistress hears about this—"

"When the headmistress owns the school, she can give the orders," the man replied. "But for now I really must insist that you let me inspect the rooms."

I could tell that Matron was taking a deep breath, the sort that she usually took just before shouting at us. But then she deflated like a burst balloon. "Fine," she said, a little more quietly. "Fine. But you will do it later; do you understand? During lesson time."

There was a moment of silence, and I thought that the man was going to argue again. But he just looked at his watch once more, and then gave a dramatic sigh. "All right. I'll go to the third floor first, then. But I will be back. I need to look at every room." And without further comment, he marched away.

Matron put her head in her hands, and she looked rather surprised when she lifted it again to find herself surrounded by a swarm of us. I had been swept along by Scarlet, but honestly I was as curious as she was.

"What's going on, Miss?" Penny demanded.

"Who was that man?" Scarlet asked.

Matron muttered something under her breath, and whatever it was, it didn't sound particularly flattering. "An inspector," she said finally. "Sent by the new owner. Wants to look around and, I don't know, measure the place or something. Well, not on my watch! Nothing goes on in these dormitories without my say-so!"

I shared a glance with Scarlet. I was fairly sure that wasn't exactly true.

There was a rush of perplexed muttering as everyone began to debate exactly what this meant. Matron looked around at all of us, and then suddenly seemed to remember exactly where she was and what was going on.

"I can't believe you lot are out of bed before the bell! I didn't think that was possible! Shoo, the lot of you!"

She waved us back into our rooms where, sure enough, the screeching bell rang out to tell us it was time to wake up.

"Bit late for that," Scarlet grumbled. "What do you think the inspector's going to do? Do you think he knows about the secret rooms?"

I frowned as I pulled my uniform from the wardrobe. "I don't know. The stairs to the ones in the basement were destroyed by the library fire, and the ones on the third floor are locked."

"And they were mostly full of broken old furniture, anyway," my twin finished. "But there could be more that we still don't know about or haven't found a way to get into. If he's so keen to poke his nose in everywhere, he'll want to know every single one, surely?"

She had a point. "Let's just hope Mrs Knight doesn't tell him anything," I said. If there were more secrets to uncover at Rookwood, then we couldn't let Henry Bartholomew be the one to find them first.

At breakfast, I wasn't entirely surprised to see Henry standing by the door to the dining hall. He had a clipboard too, with a sheaf of notes on it – presumably given to him by his inspector.

I was planning to ignore him and walk into the hall. Scarlet, though, had other ideas.

She marched straight up to him. "What are you doing?" she asked.

Henry lifted his eyes from the clipboard and smiled down at her. His teeth were white and perfect. "Hello," he said cheerfully. "Good morning to you too!"

Scarlet folded her arms and frowned at him. "Good morning? We got woken up early by *your* inspector trying to measure our rooms!"

"Mr Hardwick? Well, yes," he said, his pleasant expression not wavering. "It needs to be done, I'm afraid. I must see what state the old building is in before I decide what I want to do with it."

I tried to pull my twin away gently, but she wasn't finished.

"What about what *we* want? Does that not matter to you at all?" she demanded.

He gave a sort of quiet laugh. "Look – what's your name, girl?"

"Scarlet."

"Look, Scarlet, I wouldn't worry. This inspection is about safety. You don't want the old place falling down on your heads, do you? It's just something that has to be done." He raised his palms to the ceiling in the universal gesture for *I can't do anything about it, honest.* Then he patted her gently on the shoulder. "I'm sure whatever conclusion we come to will suit everybody."

He flashed her yet another winning smile, then walked off, hands in his pockets and whistling.

"*Hmmph,*" Scarlet said.

"What are you doing?" I asked.

She turned to me. "I wanted answers. I thought it would be easiest to get them straight from the source."

"I'm not sure that helped," I said, finally managing to drag her into the bustling dining hall.

She shook herself free of my arm. "It did no harm," she insisted. "But he didn't exactly give us anything useful. Thinks he's a charmer, clearly. But he's a snake!"

I thought about it for a moment as we pushed our way towards the serving hatch. "You think so? I mean, what if he's genuinely nice?"

She narrowed her eyes at me. "He's the son of Mr Bartholomew. You really think he's doing all this out of the goodness of his heart?"

I winced. She was probably right. But then again, shouldn't we be the first to admit that children weren't the same as their parents?

It was at that moment that Ariadne and Ebony walked in. Ariadne waved as they came over to join us in the queue. Scarlet turned to her. "Where were you two this morning?"

Ebony wrinkled her nose. "What do you mean?"

"We just woke up," Ariadne said, yawning.

I couldn't help but laugh a little at that. Ariadne was a very heavy sleeper, and she'd been up so late translating our mother's messages, I wasn't surprised that she hadn't heard the commotion.

"I was up till all hours thinking about everything from yesterday," Ebony explained. "I was sound asleep this morning."

We filled them in about the inspector and our encounter with Henry.

Ariadne tried unsuccessfully to pat down a piece of her hair that was sticking up at an odd angle. "I suppose that makes sense. He wants to see if the building is worth saving. Or whether they should knock it down and use the land to build on."

"Surely it's worth saving," Ebony said. "A place like this? It's full of history. It should be treasured." The radiator pipes beside us chose that moment to clank miserably, and a gust of wind blew the window open. Ariadne ran over to shut it.

"That's what I'm worried about, though," Scarlet told her. "That it's the history they're really after. The secrets that are here."

I didn't know if I believed that. "What if he really does just want to make money off the place? Is that better or worse?"

No one had an answer.

Several of our lessons that day were graced by the distracting presence of Mr Hardwick, the inspector. The teachers, most of them having unsuccessfully tried to shoo him away, agreed to allow him to look around each classroom. It was hard to conjugate French verbs and discuss *Oliver Twist* in English with him pottering up and down at the back of the class.

Every so often, he would stop, say "Hmm," a little too loudly, and pull out a tape measure. Next he would be scribbling notes on his clipboard, the sound of the pencil scratching in all our ears. Then he'd be kneeling to peer at the skirting board, or standing on tiptoe as he tried to examine the ceiling.

"I swear," said Scarlet during the last lesson of the day, "if he says *hmm* like that one more time, I'm going to strangle him with that bloomin' tape measure!"

I watched as Mr Hardwick went over to the fireplace at the side of the room, one of the remnants of the old house, paused, and then said, "*Hmmmmm...*"

Scarlet jumped up out of her seat, but thankfully the bell

rang right at that moment. I quickly dragged her out before she could do any damage.

The next few days continued in much the same manner. Lessons carried on as normal, and I felt almost settled back into being at school, but it was as though there was a cloud hanging over everything. We frequently glimpsed Mr Hardwick disappearing down corridors with his clipboard. Scarlet even tried to sneak a peek at what he was writing, but she came back mumbling that she couldn't read his messy scrawl.

Friday dawned with a cold fog that crept on to the school grounds. I shivered as I looked out of the window. The skeleton trees resembled charcoal sketches against the silver sky. Nonetheless, I had a good feeling about the day.

But that feeling evaporated as soon as we walked into assembly.

For a start, Mrs Knight wasn't in her usual place at the front of the stage. None of the teachers were. Instead, it was Henry Bartholomew.

"Why is he up there?" I whispered to Scarlet, but she was too busy staring at him to reply. The hall was abuzz with conversation.

"Hello, girls," he said loudly, and everyone went deadly silent. I knew they were desperate to know what he had to say. "I thought I ought to come and tell you this myself. It just seemed the right thing to do." He smiled as if he was congratulating himself.

"You *smug*—" Scarlet started to mutter under her breath, but I hit her before she could finish.

"I'm afraid my inspector has found that the school building is in need of a lot of repairs. And so it has been decided that Rookwood will shortly be closing in order to carry them out."

He paused, his eyes scanning the hall for our reaction. I expected a rush of whispers, but there was still an uneasy silence. I think we were all trying to figure out what he meant. Would the school reopen afterwards? Questions filled my head until Penny finally raised her hand. Without waiting to be called on, she asked, "Closed temporarily? Or closed permanently?"

"Ah!" Henry exclaimed, clapping his hands together and pointing back at her. "Good question. We'll be looking into the possibilities. It might be that the building would be better for another purpose. And if that's the case, then, when it closes..."

I realised that Scarlet and I were leaning forward. We were both holding our breath.

"...it might be closing its doors forever."

Chapter Eight

SCARLET

I didn't know how the teachers expected us to pay attention in lessons later that day after being hit with that bombshell in assembly. For the whole morning, they tried in vain to get us all to shut up. But it didn't work. All anyone could talk about was the school potentially closing. There was endless debate as to whether Henry would really do it, or whether it was just a possibility.

"What are we going to do?" Ariadne asked desperately that lunchtime.

I swallowed the bit of sandwich I was chewing. "I'm working on it."

The thoughts were whizzing through my brain. There had to be something we could do. I wasn't about to let our old chum *Barty* take away the one thing that was keeping Ivy and me from the clutches of our stepmother. Who did he think he was?

I just didn't have a plan. I hated not having a plan.

Ivy sighed. "Perhaps... if he really does decide to close the school, we just have to accept it, at this point."

"Absolutely not!" I told her. But deep down, a tiny part of me wondered if she was right.

Friday afternoons meant ballet, and I was looking forward to that, at least. Ivy and I ran down the chilly steps to the basement.

"Oh, hello, Scarlet," Miss Finch said. She was sitting in her usual spot at the piano. "Hello, Ivy. You're the first to arrive, once again."

"Anything to get away from the misery up there," I said, rolling my eyes.

"Well, we have some good news for you," Madame Zelda said. She was stretching her leg up on the piano, rather impressively. "Just you wait."

"Good news would certainly be welcome," said Ivy,

although she didn't seem optimistic. She still looked despondent as she sat down to lace her shoes.

I prodded her in the shoulder. "Cheer up! Good news!"

"Maybe," she said, staring at the floor.

When the whole class were present, with shoes laced and hair tied up, Madame Zelda snapped her fingers to get everyone's attention.

"Now, girls. We have an announcement for you. This year's ballet recital has been approved by the headmistress. We are going to be performing a version of the legendary *Swan Lake*."

There were lots of gasps and claps.

I looked at Ivy, my eyes wide with excitement. This had to be a good omen, didn't it? Our mother's secret music box played the theme to *Swan Lake*, and now we would get to dance in it! Not to mention that it was one of the most famous and most beautiful ballets, one in which I had always dreamt of performing. In my head I was the white swan, dancing for a packed theatre.

Madame Zelda waved her hand. "Since there were some issues with the auditions last time..." I snorted at that. Penny had been causing trouble as usual. Then Madame Boulanger, the school French teacher, had been pretending to know about ballet just because she was French (although that too was debatable given her occasional Welsh accent). It hadn't exactly worked out brilliantly. "We have decided that we will choose the roles by assessing your performance in class."

Hmm. I didn't know if that was a good thing, but I hoped it was. We'd just have to do our best in class. That would, at least, be a little less nerve-wracking than auditioning on the stage.

"But, Miss." It was Nadia raising her hand this time. "We've just been told that the school is closing! What if that happens before we can do the recital?"

Madame Zelda and Miss Finch shared a look.

"My mother has an expression, Nadia," Madame Zelda said. "It is: 'Do not try to pick the apple before you have grown the tree.'"

"What?" said Penny, her face screwed up like a pig's.

Madame Zelda sighed. "What I mean to say is that we will have to see what happens. Maybe we get apples. Maybe we get pears. Maybe we get nothing." She shrugged.

"But Nadia has a point," I replied, and it wasn't often that I said that. I could almost see my dream role disintegrating before my eyes. "We'll need a lot of time to practise and prepare. Henry Bartholomew might shut the school before we're ready."

This time Madame Zelda narrowed her eyes at me.

"Were you not listening, Scarlet? We can't be having all these *what if*s."

Miss Finch nodded slowly. "All we can do is our best. We'll have fun preparing the ballet even if we can't perform it, won't we?"

I grumbled my agreement, and looked over at Ivy. She was still staring at the floor. I could see why now. She'd realised straight away that the promise of good news was too good to be true.

And perhaps it was. But perhaps there was also something we could do about it.

Despite the looming threat of the school closure, I danced my heart out that lesson. I was determined to win a great role, even if I would never get to perform it on the stage.

But I was thinking as well. Ballet always seemed to help my brain work, to clear the cobwebs and show me the ideas I needed. And I decided that what we really needed was a new approach.

I tugged on Ivy's arm as we finished our curtsies and ended the lesson. "I'm calling an emergency meeting," I said.

"A what?" she asked.

"*An emergency meeting*," I repeated, a little louder.

She winced and held her hand over her ear. "All right! But why?"

"We need to find a way to save the school, and we can't do it alone. And I don't just mean calling Ariadne. I think we need more people. We need a team."

The look on Ivy's face told me that she wasn't quite convinced by this plan, but I could feel the wheels starting to roll. I was on to something.

"Come on," I said. "I'm starting with Penny and Nadia..."

After dinner, I stood in the darkening window of room thirteen, looking out at a small sea of confused faces.

Ivy was sitting on her bed, with Ariadne beside her. Violet and Rose were sitting on mine, talking to each other in voices so quiet that I could barely hear them. Ebony sat in the middle, on the carpet, like an island. Penny and Nadia sat a little way behind her, cross-legged.

"Right," I said. "You're probably wondering why you're all here."

"Why are we are?" Penny asked loudly.

I glared at her. "If you'll let me finish... I'm calling an emergency meeting. To save Rookwood."

I was trying to be a little dramatic, but my efforts went unnoticed.

"No," said Penny. "I meant why are *we* here." She pointed to herself and Nadia. "You hate us. I think Nadia still hates *me*."

"I don't *hate* you," said Nadia, rolling her eyes. Strangely, Penny looked quite pleased with that.

"Shut up, both of you," I said. "You're here because you're already involved, whether you like it or not. You've both been here the whole time – at Rookwood, I mean. You've seen everything that's happened with Miss Fox and Mr Bartholomew. You even read my diary!"

Nadia had the good grace to look a little sheepish about that.

But Penny just shrugged. "I still don't get it."

"All right," I said to her. "You want me to speak your language? Henry is a snake. It takes one to know one."

"Huh!" she said. "Well, perhaps you've got a point there." She was clearly trying to look annoyed, but her face soon broke into a devious grin.

"Right, then," I said, clasping my hands together. "I think I should explain about the Whispers in the Walls. Some of you already know, but not all of you."

There were a few knowing nods from my friends, while those who didn't know what I was talking about looked puzzled.

"The Whispers was a secret group that our mother was part of, many years ago. We found out about them when Violet hid Rose in a concealed room in the basement that had their writing all over the wall."

Ebony's mouth dropped open. "Wait, what? There's a hidden room in the basement?"

"Not any more," Ariadne said. "The entrance was destroyed in a fire."

"And why was Rose hiding in it?" Ebony asked.

"Because Violet rescued her from an asylum, and her family were trying to kill her," I said.

"Oh," said Ebony.

"So anyway, the Whispers' aim was to expose the original Mr Bartholomew for his cruelty," I continued, "and for the punishment he gave to a pupil that led to her death."

Ebony had really missed out on a lot of the dramatic events at Rookwood.

Nadia raised her hand. "I heard he stabbed her with a letter opener."

I sighed. "No. He didn't. But anyway, we managed to track down all this information that the Whispers had, and we used it to trick him into confessing."

Now Violet raised her hand. "I don't understand where this is going."

I glared at her. "You don't need to keep raising your hands. Just listen to me, all right? The Whispers never managed to take down Mr Bartholomew, but *we* helped their voices be heard. Now we're up against his son, and the school is about to be closed – whether that's really temporary or not. And the thing is, thanks to Ariadne translating the secret code, Ivy and I have found some new information left by our mother."

"What information?" Violet asked.

I put my head in my hands. This was like herding cats. Luckily, Ivy took over for me. "She was investigating the headmaster on her own too, after she left school. She'd heard rumours that he didn't truly own Rookwood."

Several mouths dropped open.

"But that would mean..." Rose whispered.

"Exactly," I told them. "If the rumours are true, then it would mean that Henry Bartholomew doesn't really own it either. And if we can prove that, we can save the school."

Penny wrinkled her nose, making her freckles join together. "And how exactly are we supposed to do that?"

I took a deep breath. "By working together. I'm proposing that we form a new Whispers in the Walls. And this time, we're going to succeed."

Chapter Nine

IVY

Scarlet's suggestion was met with a buzz of conversation. Most of the others still looked a little perplexed. Ariadne started clapping, only to trail off when she realised that no one else was joining her.

"Hang on, hang on," Penny started. She stood up and waved her arms at everyone else. "Shut up for a minute!" She looked back at Scarlet. "What's so great about Rookwood, exactly? This place is a dump. Even Henry thinks so. I wouldn't be surprised if he's going to scrap the school entirely. What's the point in us coming up with some complicated plan to save it?"

Scarlet paused in exasperated silence before continuing. "Look. In the first form I would have agreed with you. Rookwood was awful. Miss Fox was terrifying. But now? It's finally getting better! And we've all got friends here. I can't imagine going to a school where we wouldn't be together."

Violet nodded her agreement. "It's so much better here than it was." She had been in the first form with Scarlet as well, before Miss Fox had had them both locked in the asylum. "And my legal guardian is... well... not the best. I fought to come back here. I couldn't leave Rose on her own, could I?"

Scarlet pointed at her. "Yes! Exactly."

Rose nodded. "I have nowhere else to go," she whispered.

"And, Penny," Scarlet said. "Aren't your parents splitting up? Do you really want to go back to that?"

Penny narrowed her eyes, and I braced myself for her to start shouting at Scarlet, but instead she sank back down. "Point taken," she said dejectedly.

"This is our home," Scarlet said. "Whether we like it or not. We can make it something good – great, even – or we can lose it and lose all our friends, and end up back with our parents, or, or... locked in an asylum!"

I could see what Penny meant about the school, but I could also see Scarlet's point of view. "Our stepmother will kill us if we get sent home," I said. "Even if Rookwood is awful... it's the best alternative."

Ariadne put her hand up. Scarlet turned to her. "What now?"

Ariadne stood and said, a bit sheepishly, "Actually, I really like Rookwood."

Nobody was sure what to say to that.

"Well, I like learning—" Ariadne began.

"Because you're a giant swot," Penny interrupted, but the rest of us shushed her.

Ariadne frowned at her. "But it's not just that. Rookwood is about freedom to me. I know it seems like we're trapped, but... it's nothing compared to how I felt at home, or at my last school. There's so much I can do here. And I have my friends and we go on adventures and..." Her eyes started to water, and she sniffed. "I think it's worth saving."

There was a long pause, and eventually Scarlet took charge again.

"Who's with me, then?" she said.

Ariadne's hand shot up. I raised mine, and as I looked around, I saw everyone else follow suit.

Penny was the last, and she lifted her hand in the most

half-hearted way possible. "Fine," she said. "It'll give me something to do."

Scarlet clapped her hands. "Excellent. Now we just need a plan..."

By the end of the meeting, we had a page torn from Scarlet's diary, written by Ariadne, that looked like this:

THE NEW WHISPERS IN THE WALLS

Chairwoman: Scarlet Grey
Secretary and codebreaker: Ariadne
Elizabeth Gwendolyn Flitworth

Members:
Ivy Grey
Rose Fitzwarren
Violet Adams
Ebony McCloud
Nadia Sayani
Penny Winchester

Ariadne's role was self-appointed, and there had been some argument about Scarlet being the chairwoman. But she'd won by pointing out that the entire thing was her idea and that most of them hadn't even wanted to join a few minutes earlier. And then there was another page that read:

THE PLAN

1. Scarlet, Ivy and Ariadne - investigate Rookwood's history at the library

2. Penny and Nadia - keep an eye on H. Report back on his activities

3. Rose and Violet - look for any evidence of hidden rooms etc.

4. Ebony - get her father to find out what he can. Could he help out with money?

We'd decided against writing the entire thing in code, since it would take too long. At least we had a safe hiding place for what we'd written – inside the secret compartment of the music box, alongside our mother's notes.

"Right," Scarlet said. She was clearly enjoying being the

boss a bit too much. "Let's see how we get on with this over the weekend and meet again on Sunday evening."

At that moment, there was a knock at the door, and all of us jumped. Nadia, who was nearest, got up to answer it.

It was Matron, hands on hips. "What are you lot up to in here?" she asked suspiciously.

Nadia, without missing a beat, said, "Oh, hello, Matron. We were just discussing the ballet recital. We're so excited for it, you see. We need to get lots of practice!"

Matron's frown blossomed into a smile. "Oh, well, that's rather lovely. Come along, though, you all need to be getting ready for bed now. Teeth brushed! Nightgowns on!"

She ushered the other girls out of our room.

"Sunday!" Scarlet shouted after them. "Next... ballet meeting!"

I couldn't help but giggle at her. "Half of them don't even do ballet," I whispered.

"Matron doesn't know that," said Scarlet, and she grinned at me.

I went to bed that night feeling a little more confident. Even in the darkness and the cold, there was a spark of hope.

We rushed through breakfast on Saturday morning so that we could get to the library. There had to be *something* we could find in there about the school's history.

We got there so early that Miss Jones the librarian was only just opening up. She was yawning as she went behind the desk. "Gosh, girls, you're keen," she said. "Jing isn't even here yet." Jing was Miss Jones's niece, and the head helper at the library since Anna Santos had proved to be a little useless.

"We're investigating again, Miss," Ariadne said in her usual bright and cheerful way, which made Miss Jones freeze to the spot.

"Are you looking into what's going on with the school?" she said, keeping her voice low and looking around warily. "And *Henry Bartholomew*?" she asked, apparently reassured that he wasn't about to jump out at us.

We nodded.

"Please be careful," she begged us. "It's dangerous."

Miss Jones had turned out to be the key witness to what Mr Bartholomew had done to our mother's best friend, Emmeline. It seemed she thought Henry was likely to be as bad as his father.

"Don't worry," Scarlet reassured her, leaning forward over the desk. "It's nothing. Just a bit of a history lesson."

The librarian nodded, but she still looked a little pale. "All right. What do you need?"

"What do you have on Rookwood's history?" I asked.

"Ah." Miss Jones winced. "Not much, I'm afraid. We lost

a lot in the fire. There were only a few documents that survived. Come on, I'll show you." She beckoned us to follow her, and then trotted off into the stacks, to one of the sections that had been fitted with new shelves.

One of them was marked LOCAL HISTORY and contained several wooden boxes, all of which were shut.

"Hmm, it should be..." She ran her finger along the numbers on the edge of the shelf. "Ah."

She picked up one of the boxes, and we heard a heavy *thud* as the shelf came loose, the boxes sliding down before finally coming to a halt at the edge.

"Um," Ariadne said.

Miss Jones remained silent for a moment, and then I could have sworn she muttered something about "*Lousy cheap rubbish,*" and "*the whole place is falling apart,*" before turning round. "Never mind! I'll get that fixed," she said. "Have a look through this one. It's all we have left, unfortunately."

She thrust the box into Scarlet's hands and hurried away, presumably to find the caretaker.

We found a quiet table in a corner and emptied the contents of the box out on to it.

There were a couple of slightly crumpled maps with yellowing edges, a few similarly old-looking sheets of paper with lists of names and dates on, and some more pages of writing whose contents I couldn't discern at first glance.

"Is that all that's in there?" Ariadne asked.

Scarlet shook the box over the table. A few specks of dust fell out, followed by a small spider that hastily scurried away. "Yep," she said.

I sat down with a sigh. "Well, it's something. Let's take a look."

Together we combed through the files. I took the maps, Ariadne took the lists and Scarlet took the miscellaneous writing. Wordlessly, Ariadne handed us both magnifying glasses.

"Where did you get...?" Scarlet began. "Actually, never mind. I should just assume you bring *everything* to school from now on."

Ariadne grinned at her.

The library was still and quiet around us, even more so than usual. You could see the motes of dust in the morning sunlight from the tall windows, and the air smelt pleasantly of books.

The maps I had were of Rookwood, that much was clear. The first one I looked at was relatively recent, from maybe only a few decades earlier, and showed the school. The classrooms and dorms had all been painstakingly labelled, and as far as I could tell everything seemed the same as I knew it. But this map showed no sign of any of the secret rooms that we'd discovered. The whole third floor was just marked as Out of Bounds. The only difference that I could see was that Matron's apartment had been marked with a set of initials: EMW.

I wrote the initials down in my notebook, wondering what they stood for.

The second map was older, drawn in ink so ancient that it had faded to brown. The handwriting was curlier and harder to read, but I could tell that the label at the top read *Rookwood House*.

"Ah," I said aloud. "This one is of the house before it became a school. Could be useful."

"I've got lists of... servants, I think," Ariadne said, looking up at me over the table. "Chambermaid, butler, groundskeeper... and their salaries. Some of them are crossed out."

Scarlet raised an eyebrow. "Is that relevant?"

"Hmm." Ariadne stared down at the paper again. "It depends when this is from, but possibly..." She went quiet.

Scarlet flipped over a page impatiently. "I'm not even sure what this is. I can barely read it. I think they might be more of the same documents that our mother found."

"Keep trying," I encouraged her, looking back at my map. I was sure there would be something of interest there.

First I tried to look for rooms I knew. The hall where we had assembly was labelled as a ballroom, while the library still appeared to be a library. The upstairs, though, looked completely different.

Rather than our pokey dorms, it was laid out as large bedrooms set alongside a long walking gallery. Only one of those grand bedrooms seemed to have remained as it was – the one that was now Matron's apartment, and had been labelled EMW on the newer map. I noticed there was some sort of square marked in the corner of it.

I made a note of that too.

Ariadne leant over and looked at what I'd written. "Oh gosh!" she said suddenly. "I think I've got it!"

Chapter Ten

SCARLET

Ariadne's exclamation was welcome, because I was getting utterly fed up of attempting to read the ancient swirly writing on my pages and not getting anywhere. All I'd picked out was the word *Wootton*, the name Ariadne had told us had belonged to the original owners of the house. I could hardly tell what the rest of it said.

"What is it?" I asked our friend.

"I think this proves your mother was right," she said, standing up and looking back and forth between what she and Ivy had laid out. "Well, perhaps it's not *concrete* proof."

I folded my arms and gave her an impatient look.

"All right, all right!" she protested. "I think this 'EMW' –" she tapped Ivy's map – "was Eliza Mary Wootton, the last Lady of Rookwood."

"Could be," said Ivy. "But why would she be on this newer map of the school?"

Ariadne tapped her pen against her lip thoughtfully. "From what I read, she was still present in the house when the school started running. She might even have been the real founder of the school, and Mr Bartholomew just stole her thunder."

"Hmmph," I said. "I wouldn't put it past him."

"Yes," Ariadne continued, "and the thing was that Lady Wootton was running out of money. You can see all the servants getting crossed off the list on the final page. I think she ended up turning the house into a school to try to make money. She must have been very old at that point, though, so it would appear she hired Mr Bartholomew to run it."

"That was a bit of a mistake," said Ivy, putting it mildly.

"He probably bumped her off," I said. Talking about the old headmaster always left a bitter taste in my mouth. He had been such a despicable person. "If she had no children, he could easily have made a claim and then fabricated the evidence to pretend he'd been entitled to it all along."

Ariadne nodded and pointed to her list again. "But look – this list is from Lady Wootton's time, and what do you notice?"

Ivy peered at it and began to read aloud. "Butler, groundskeeper, nursemaid, governess..." She stopped and looked up at us both, the realisation dawning in her eyes. "She had children!"

"Exactly!" Ariadne clapped her hands with glee and bounced on the spot.

"So Mr Bartholomew lied about owning Rookwood. It should have been inherited by her children," I said, dropping my pen on the table in disgust. "What a surprise."

"But what happened to them?" Ivy asked.

I rolled my eyes. "He probably killed them too."

Ariadne shrugged. "There's no way to tell from this. But it was a long time ago, before the turn of the century." Her expression turned a little sad. "They could have died of an illness, or in an accident."

I shoved the papers I'd been reading towards her. "Perhaps Miss Jones will let you take this lot out, and you can try to decipher them. You're much better at solving these things than I am." I turned back to Ivy. "Anything else from the old map?"

There was a short silence as she pored over it for a while longer. "I think this might have been the map that the

Whispers looked at, and that Violet used when she was trying to find somewhere to hide Rose. It shows the basement, and you can just about see that there is – was – a door leading down to it from the library. That must be how they discovered it. But the whole thing is just labelled as CELLAR. You can't really tell where everything is."

There were several basement-level rooms that we knew about: the secret one that was no longer accessible, the vaulted room that was now the ballet studio, and the wine cellar below the kitchens that was accessed either by a locked door or, if you were sneaky, by climbing into the dumbwaiter. The basement on the map appeared far bigger than all of those rooms put together – it looked pretty much the size of the entire school.

"It must be a maze down there," I said.

"We don't know how much of it was used for anything, though," Ariadne pointed out. "And whatever it was in the past, half of it could be caved in, for all we know."

"This is useless," I said. "This stuff might confirm our mother's suspicions to us, but what can we really do with it? None of this is real proof. We're not going to get rid of Henry that easily."

Ivy and Ariadne looked at me, but neither of them said anything.

"Come on," I said. "Let's put it all back. We'll tell

everyone what we've found at the meeting. Perhaps they'll have some ideas…"

*

By the time Sunday evening rolled around, I was itching to get the next Whispers meeting started. We were armed with our new knowledge, baffling though it might be, and we'd ventured out to the shops in Rookwood village so that Ariadne could stock up on sweets. We were ready.

After Rookwood's traditional Sunday Stew (or rather, traditional Every Day Stew) we raced back up to room thirteen. At least, thanks to Nadia, we now had a good cover story for why we were gathering so many girls in our room. We just had to hope that Matron didn't think to investigate our "ballet practice" any further.

Ariadne had managed to persuade Jing to let us sneak the box of papers out of the library by bribing her with a sugar mouse, so we spread them on the carpet for the others to look at. "Just don't get them sticky," she warned us. "I need to get them back in perfect condition!"

Ebony, Rose and Violet were the first to arrive, followed by Penny and Nadia.

"I officially call this meeting of the new Whispers in the Walls to order," I began.

"How come *you* get to call the meeting to order?" Penny asked.

"Because it's *my* secret organisation!" I said. "Keep up! Right, let's get started..."

I let Ivy and Ariadne explain the documents and maps that we'd found, and how they indicated that our mother had been right – Mr Bartholomew probably had taken Rookwood from an old lady, and probably through (as Ariadne put it) "nefarious means".

"But that's all we've got," I said, sitting down on my bed and swinging my legs. "Nothing solid. Anyone else?" I glanced down at our plan. "Penny and Nadia, any luck with the spying?"

Penny had a mouthful of sweets at this point, so Nadia stood up. "Not really," she said. "Henry was in the school yesterday, so we tried to follow him together. He spent a lot of time in Mrs Knight's office. Honestly, it was very boring."

"Did he go anywhere else?" Ivy asked.

Nadia began braiding a strand of her hair as she thought about it. "He met up with his inspector man, and they went upstairs."

Penny gulped down her sweets. "The third floor."

Nadia nodded. "I think they wanted to look around up here, too, but Matron glared at them until they went away."

"Ha!" I said. "Good old Matron. Okay, so that doesn't get us very far."

"They seem to be very interested in the building," Ebony

said. She was sitting beside Rose and Violet. "Maybe they think there's something here. Hidden treasure, perhaps... A book of spells—"

"Oh, don't start that again," Penny snapped.

Violet shot a glare at Penny. "Ebony has a point. They're up to something. Why would they need to keep looking around so much? Why does it matter what's in the building if they're just going to knock it down and start again?"

I nodded and chewed the inside of my lip. Henry and his inspector were searching the school, it seemed. But for what? "Well, my theory was that they were looking for the secret rooms, but I don't know what good that would do them." I gestured to Violet and Rose. "So did you find anything?"

Rose whispered something in Violet's ear, and whatever it was, Violet seemed to agree. "We did our best. We thought we'd try and see if there was any way back down into the basement. We tried pushing on all the bookcases in the library, just in case. But nothing happened."

"Henry didn't seem that interested in the basement, anyway," Nadia pointed out. "He mostly looked upstairs, when he wasn't interrogating Mrs Knight."

"Right," Violet continued. "And when Rose and I were going down there, we did look to see if there were any other ways in or out, and we couldn't find any. Although that doesn't mean they don't exist, I suppose." She sighed. "And upstairs, well... everything's locked."

I sighed too. "It was all broken furniture when we looked up there, but it was where we found the Whispers' code book..." Quite honestly, I doubted that there was anything useful on the third floor.

"I could pick the locks," Ariadne suggested. It was one of her many strange talents.

Rose looked unconvinced, and Violet just frowned. "There are tons of doors up there. You could spend all week picking locks and not find a shred of useful information."

Ariadne's shoulders sagged. "True. Perhaps as a last resort?"

Now Violet turned to Ebony. "Looks like you're our only hope," she said. Ebony's father owned the local theatre and was fairly well off and well connected. He'd donated money to the school in the past, which had all the teachers fawning over him.

Every face in the room turned eagerly to Ebony, but our hopes sank when she shrugged. "I don't think my father can help."

"Rats," Ariadne said. Her pen had been eagerly poised over her paper, but she dropped it to the carpet. "What did he say?"

"I didn't get much out of him," she explained. "I had to pretend to Mrs Knight that I had a family emergency so that she would let me telephone him. I couldn't hear very well... He said he was busy with the theatre's new production of *Romeo and Juliet*, and I didn't get much of a chance to explain..." She started fiddling with the laces of her black boots.

"Out with it," Penny demanded. "What did he say about helping the school?"

"He said he couldn't spare the time at the moment, and that he thought I hated the school anyway after what I did last term." Ebony rolled her eyes.

"Well," Ariadne said sheepishly. "You did pretend to be a witch to try and get expelled, and you—"

"All right, yes, Ariadne, we know," I said as Ebony started to blush.

The conversation went round in circles a few more times. When I finally concluded the meeting (by telling them all to shut up, naturally), I took a look at what Ariadne had written on the list.

WHAT WE KNOW

1. Scarlet, Ivy and Ariadne - Eliza Mary Wootton was the last Lady of Rookwood. She probably had children. Ran out of money and opened her house as a school run by Mr B, while she lived in what is now Matron's apartment. Mr B then somehow took control of the school and claimed he had always owned it.

2. Penny and Nadia - Henry and his inspector seem to be looking for something at the school. Focusing on the upper floors. Maybe secret rooms?

3. Rose and Violet - No luck finding more secret rooms. Another way into the basement? Could be more on third floor - is it worth picking the locks?

4. Ebony - Her father can't (won't?) help.

Hopeless!

I resisted the urge to bang my head against the wall. I'd really hoped that with everyone teaming up, we would defeat Henry easily. Instead, we didn't seem to be getting anywhere. And Rookwood was running out of time.

I turned to Ivy as everyone was leaving. "We need a miracle," I said.

Chapter Eleven

IVY

Something about Scarlet's words stuck in my head. I spent the night thinking over what we'd found – about what might have happened to the Lady of Rookwood or her children, and how we could ever find out, when it happened so long ago. Was every piece of evidence gone? Were there secret places we didn't know about that held forgotten relics of the past, or was that all in our imagination?

If we lost Rookwood, I felt like we'd be losing the

connection to our mother. We had to finish the fight that she'd started.

We did need a miracle.

But as for where you found a miracle, I didn't know.

Until I fell into a fretful sleep, and a dream began...

I was walking through Rookwood. At first, I thought that I had just climbed out of bed and gone walking to the lavatories, but everything seemed strange. A dim light glimmered on the walls above me as if reflected underwater. And the corridor seemed to stretch on and on for miles.

After what seemed like an age, I began to see a door. It was familiar, but I wasn't sure why. It got smaller and smaller, and I felt like Alice falling down the rabbit hole. By the time I reached the door, it was only waist height. I pulled it open, but it contained only darkness.

Still, for some reason, I knew it was the place I had to go. I crawled inside. Immediately the walls began to move, and the whole thing shifted and creaked. Eventually, the door burst open and I tumbled out into an empty room.

Wait, no – the room wasn't empty. There was a shadow there, in one corner. A shadow of a person, but I couldn't recognise their face.

In a voice like the static from a wireless, the shadow spoke. "What do you need?"

I fished around in my memory and found Scarlet's words. I swallowed. "A miracle. Please."

The shadow tipped its head on one side as if it were considering this. "Miracles are hard to come by," it said at last. "What's the opposite of a miracle?"

Was this a riddle? I didn't understand. I began to feel afraid. "A curse?" I tried.

Although I couldn't see the shadow's expression, I got the sense that it was smiling. "When there are no angels to be found, perhaps you need to turn to the devils."

"What does that mean?" I asked, but the shadow was already disappearing, slipping into the floor. "Wait! Don't—" I leapt forward, tried to catch it by the hand, but it was made of nothingness, and suddenly I was falling, until...

The real world came rushing back in a blaze of sunlight, and a cacophony of wind and birdsong. I scrabbled at my bedsheets and sat up, blinking rapidly.

When I was finally certain I was awake, I turned to see what was going on. To my surprise, Scarlet was leaning half out of the open window, craning her neck upwards.

"Scarlet!" I jumped out of bed, grabbed the back of her

nightgown and pulled her back in. "What on earth are you doing?"

She pushed me away. "Investigating," she said, with more than a little indignation.

"But the morning bell hasn't even gone yet!" I said.

"Hmmph." My twin sat down on her bed. "I just had an idea, that's all. I thought we might be able to climb into the rooms upstairs from the outside."

My mouth dropped open. "You can't be serious. How is that better than lock picking? And you'd still have to smash the window; don't you think someone would notice?"

"S'pose," she replied, now looking sheepish. "It was just a thought."

I wrenched the window shut before any more freezing air could spill in. "Don't you remember what happened to Josephine? You saw her after she was pushed out of that window. And she got off lightly." My chest finally stopped heaving.

"All right, all right! Sorry! No more hanging out of windows!" Scarlet rolled her eyes. "But look, I'm at my wits' end here. We have to find some way to keep the investigation going. I'm not going to *lose*."

My twin was a sore loser at the best of times, let alone when our school and our mother's legacy were at stake. And I had to admit, I felt the same.

Henry's words seemed decent enough, but was he a true Bartholomew underneath? Did he really care what he was doing to Rookwood? To all of us? If he had more dastardly plans, I wanted us to be the ones to foil them.

Scarlet sighed and began to get dressed, and I followed suit.

"*We need a miracle,*" she muttered again under her breath.

The echo of the dream came to my mind once more, but it was interrupted by the clanging of the morning bell. There was a thought forming, but it had gone as soon as it had arrived.

For the rest of the day, I felt as though I were slipping through the lessons without quite being there. It was like trying to remember something on the tip of your tongue. I kept trying to replay the dream, but now I wasn't sure if I'd remembered it exactly right.

I was almost given a detention for daydreaming, so Scarlet took it upon herself to keep jabbing me with her pen every time I looked like I wasn't paying attention. Ariadne kept asking if I was all right, and I told her I just hadn't had enough sleep. I didn't know how to explain what I was feeling.

That was – until I got to ballet.

"Miss Finch is a little late today," Madame Zelda said, her lips pursed. I think Madame Zelda thought that lateness was some sort of crime. Whenever anyone was late she would usually tap her long fingers on her arm relentlessly until they entered, and then shout, "WHAT TIME DO YOU CALL THIS?"

Today she did the finger-tapping, but she thankfully didn't shout at Miss Finch when she finally arrived. She just gave her a look of perplexed anger and carried on instructing us on our *demi-pliés*.

Something about the sound of Miss Finch's walking stick on the stone steps brought my mind into focus.

"*Perhaps you need to turn to the devils...*" I muttered, remembering my dream. Scarlet looked at me as if I'd gone completely mad.

We had a few moments to ourselves as Madame Zelda hurried over to Miss Finch and began to talk to her under her breath. Miss Finch looked flustered and apologetic. I hoped she was all right.

But I thought I knew, then. I thought I knew what the dream was trying to tell me. What my own mind was trying to tell me. It was an idea, and it was a terrible one.

That was the choice I had: a terrible idea, or no ideas at all.

"What's wrong with you?" Scarlet whispered in my ear. "You look like you've seen a ghost!"

I turned back to my twin. "I've had an idea," I said. "But you're not going to like it..."

Chapter Twelve

SCARLET

Ivy wouldn't tell me her idea for the rest of the lesson. "Not here," she kept saying, shaking her head. We were busy practising for *Swan Lake* anyway, and I was trying desperately to out-dance everyone else, but I was more than a little distracted by what Ivy had said.

What could possibly be so bad? I was no stranger to bad ideas. After all, I'd been the one hanging out of our dorm-room window this morning.

I pestered her about it all the way back to the room.

"All right!" she said finally when we were through the

door. She tossed her *pointe* shoes on the bed, which was a little unlike her, but I had to admit I had been quite annoying. "I'll tell you my idea!"

"Finally." I crossed my arms. "Come on, then."

She took a deep breath. "I think we need to talk to Miss Fox."

"WHAT?" I exclaimed, so loudly that I swear the window rattled.

Her expression said it all. She *knew* it was a terrible idea. "I know," she said. "But I had this dream, and—"

"A *dream*?" I gaped at her.

She waved her hand dismissively. "Forget the dream. It doesn't matter. The point is, Miss Fox taught here for years. She probably knew Mr Bartholomew better than anyone. She might have known what he was up to. I mean, she hated him, didn't she? She'd probably be happy to get some revenge, and—"

I grabbed her shoulders. I wanted to shake some sense into her. "Ivy. This is *Miss Fox* we're talking about – the one who's locked up in prison for attempted murder! She tried to *kill us*! What are you suggesting? That we just waltz in there and ask her for a cup of tea and a chat?"

"No –" Ivy's cheeks burned red as she shook me off – "but perhaps there's a way we could get information out of her—"

"She's in *prison*!" I repeated. "And we don't even know where!"

But my twin just wasn't getting the message. "We can talk to Miss Finch. She's Miss Fox's daughter, after all. She might know."

I rolled my eyes. "Oh, wonderful. *'Hello, Miss Finch, remember your evil mother who you didn't see for years and who then kidnapped you and locked you in a tower? Are you still good friends?'*"

Ivy glared at me. "You said we need a miracle. I know this is a long shot, but it's still... something. Something is better than nothing."

I turned away from her, my chest heaving. "We're not doing it. End of discussion."

"Then we'll lose the school and we'll be sent straight back to our stepmother! Because we have nothing else!" she said. She darted back in front of me, so I couldn't avoid her eye. "Think about it, Scarlet. What if we can get Miss Fox to admit that she bribed our stepmother as well, that she got her to pretend you were dead? We could kill two birds with one stone!"

"And probably get killed ourselves!" I retorted. "Miss Fox is a monster. And *if* she doesn't kill us, *if* we even find her, how will we make her tell us anything?"

Ivy's eyebrows knitted. "I don't know. Perhaps Miss Finch could help us."

"There you go again." This idea got worse and worse the

more I heard. Surely Miss Finch wanted nothing to do with her mother, after everything she'd done?

"I think it might be our only chance," my twin said. "I can't stop thinking about it. If our mother was right about Mr Bartholomew taking over the school by illicit means, Miss Fox might well be the only person that knows the truth."

I clicked my fingers. "What about Madame Lovelace? She's as old as the hills. Why don't we ask *her*?" Our history teacher had given us some information in the past, although it was usually a bit vague.

Now Ivy looked as exasperated with me as I was with her. "Madame Lovelace barely remembers anything that happened after eighteen ninety-nine!"

I threw my hands up in frustration. "Well, I don't see why we can't ask—"

"Fine," Ivy said. "We'll ask her tomorrow. But I need you to think about my idea. We should consider it. Even if it's the last resort."

I took a deep, shuddering breath, my face burning. Even the mention of Miss Fox's name made me feel sick. I didn't want to have anything more to do with her, for as long as I lived. But the way Ivy was looking at me – she really meant it. She really thought this was our only hope.

Through gritted teeth, I said, "Maybe. *Maybe*. But we'll

talk to the Whispers about it first. We'll talk about *considering it.*"

"All right," she said, sitting down heavily on the carpet. "That's enough."

We didn't talk for the rest of the night. Ivy didn't even dare raise the idea with Ariadne and the others at dinner, but I told them to come to our dorm again the next evening for another Whispers meeting. I went to bed silently fuming, but deep down I was afraid. I was too afraid even to write the words in my diary.

If I wanted my twin to talk to me again, I knew I was going to have to let her tell everyone her idea. But I didn't even want to entertain it. I knew better than anybody that you didn't mess with Miss Fox. We needed to stay far, far away from her, or we were putting our lives in her hands.

I pulled the covers up over my head and squeezed my eyes tightly shut. But no matter how hard I tried, I couldn't shake off the memories of jangling keys and a cane swishing through the air.

I woke up the next day feeling more resolved. I wasn't going to let Ivy (or anyone else, for that matter) push me around. If I wanted to be the only sane one and stay away from Miss Fox, then that was what was going to happen.

I had a shred of hope for the Madame Lovelace idea too. Maybe she really would be able to give us something useful.

"Morning," I said to Ivy, testing the waters.

"Morning," she said back, with a delicate smile.

So the fight was resolved. For now... Who knew what the meeting would bring?

At breakfast, Ariadne showed us her notes on the squiggly documents that I hadn't been able to make any sense of. "I didn't get very far," she told us. "The handwriting is impossible. I'm fairly sure it's more about the history of the building and the Woottons. But at the very end there was suddenly a mention of it becoming Rookwood School, and the initials EB."

I didn't even have to think about it. "Edgar Bartholomew."

Ariadne nodded. "But what does it all mean?"

"No idea. He probably added it himself to make his takeover of the school seem more legitimate." I pushed my porridge around with my spoon. "I think I'm going to try Madame Lovelace."

Ebony looked up from her breakfast, her face lined with confusion. "The history teacher?"

I nodded. "She's ancient. Almost a fossil. We talked to her before about our mother and our aunt, about when they were at the school."

"Oh," Ebony replied. "So you think she'll know about what Mr Bartholomew did?"

"If she knew at the time," Ivy interjected, "she's probably forgotten it by now."

I put my spoon down on the table with a *clang*. "Well, we're trying it." *And it's a much better idea than yours*, I didn't add.

We endured a boring lesson on the Boer Wars, while I sat at my desk itching to ask about the school's past. Why couldn't we learn things like that in history – things that were actually useful and relevant?

Madame Lovelace, shockingly, had managed to stay awake for the entire time, and now that everyone was rushing out, she was sitting slumped in her chair. As always she was covered in a fine layer of chalk dust, even over her glasses.

I told the others I'd meet them later, so eventually it was only Ivy and me left in the classroom. I thought we might have more chance of getting her to talk than if there was a big group of us.

I sidled up to the history teacher. "Madame Lovelace?"

She blinked slowly and looked up at me. "Mm?"

I cleared my throat. "You've been here forty years, haven't you?"

She smiled, and I noticed some of her teeth were missing. "Oh yes. It feels like only yesterday I came to teach here." She took her glasses off and rubbed them on her dress, getting them even dustier in the process. "Why, I remember arriving in the horse-drawn carriage, with old Albert, I think his name was, and hearing the rooks cawing at me from up on the chimney breasts – and back in those days we still lit all the fires, so the smoke filled the air and—"

"Yes, right," I interrupted, hoping to divert the river of conversation away from nostalgic rambling and towards something useful. "But what do you know about the origins of the school?"

"Ah, well," she said, "it was a grand old house, of course, the ancestral home of the Woottons, the Lords of Rookwood. But most of the family met a sad fate. When they were all gone but one, it became a school..."

I knew I was being impatient, but we already knew all of this. By now, Ivy was eyeing the door, obviously thinking this was going nowhere. So I stopped the history teacher again. "Actually, it was something more specific we wanted to ask about. Do you think Mr Bartholomew could have stolen the school from the Woottons?"

Madame Lovelace's grey eyes went cold, and the colour drained from her face. "We shall not speak of that man," she said.

"But, Miss—" Ivy tried.

It was no use. Madame Lovelace tutted, pursed her lips and closed the books on her desk shut with a bang. "Dark deeds," she muttered. "I shall not speak of this any more."

And with that, she rose from her chair and shuffled out of the classroom – leaving us once again without any hope of answers.

Chapter Thirteen

IVY

Although our history teacher's reaction had been a little strange, it was understandable. Mr Bartholomew had not been a pleasant man. "Dark deeds," she had said – did she mean what he had done to the Woottons, or what he had done to our mother's best friend, or a hundred other things besides? Whatever the answer, it was all equally awful.

But we needed that information if we had any possibility of saving the school, and now we were out of options. All the options, that is, except for the most horrible: going to speak to Miss Fox.

Scarlet had reluctantly told all of the new Whispers to meet in our room once again, so that we could discuss it. I could tell she was secretly hoping that everyone would hate the idea as much as she did. Truth be told, I hated it too. The idea of seeing Miss Fox again filled me with terror just as it did my twin.

The other option, though, was potentially losing the school. Losing everything we'd gained over the last couple of years – our friendships, our newfound strength, our last real connection to our mother's life. I felt we'd be back at square one, only worse, because our father was forgetting us and our stepmother would have us thrown in the asylum.

I held the door open as the others trooped into our room. Matron caught sight of us from the corridor. "More ballet practice, girls?" she asked. "I do admire your work ethic."

Nadia gave her a nod and a curtsey.

"Thank you, Miss," I said, more than a little sheepishly. I didn't enjoy lying, but I knew Matron wouldn't allow us to have our meetings otherwise. She smiled and bustled away towards her room.

"Right," said Penny, once we were all inside. "What is it this time? Did you actually find anything useful?"

I was expecting Scarlet to shout at her, but instead my

twin sat down on the floor, folded her arms and looked up at me. "I'm letting Ivy handle this one," she said, "since it's her terrible idea."

"Thanks," I huffed. "Look, I know it *sounds* bad. But if you just think about it—"

"It doesn't sound like anything to us," Nadia pointed out, "because we have no idea what your idea is."

I ran a hand through my hair and tried to calm myself down. It was hard even to say the words. "All right, well... now that we've investigated in every way we can think of, and we're just hitting dead ends at every turn... I think it's time for a last resort—" I was faltering.

"And?" my twin interrupted, waving me on.

"I think we should talk to Miss Fox," I said, the whole thing coming out in a rush.

"WHAT?" Violet exclaimed.

"Are you *serious*?" Penny said, her mouth dropping open.

"Why?" asked Ariadne.

They all started shouting objections and questions over the top of each other. I stood there helplessly until Scarlet yelled at them to give me a chance – though it didn't escape my notice that she'd left it just long enough for me to get a good idea of how badly this idea was going down.

When they'd finally stopped, I began to explain. "We've

run out of other options. But Miss Fox, well, she was here a long time. She knew the secrets of the school – she had the keys to every room in the place, didn't she? And she knew Mr Bartholomew, enough to be terrified of him."

"And Ivy thinks Miss Fox might be happy to help us out because she'd like to get revenge on that old ogre, alive or dead," Scarlet added, although there was more than a hint of disdain in her voice.

I took a deep breath. "Yes. And I think Miss Finch would be able to get us to her – she would know where her mother is being kept, surely."

"I don't have the faintest idea what you're talking about," Ebony piped up.

Violet turned to her. "Miss Fox? Former headmistress? Evil? Had Scarlet and me thrown in an asylum to cover up that Miss Finch was her secret child?"

Ebony nodded slowly. "Right... And Rose?" She pointed. "Did she have Rose thrown in there too?"

Rose shook her head. She had gone a little pale at the mention of Miss Fox. I supposed she had witnessed Miss Fox's reign of mysterious terror last year, and Violet had probably filled her in.

"Oh no," Violet explained. "I just met Rose in the asylum. She was sent there by her nasty cousins who wanted to keep her away from the inheritance."

"I see," said Ebony, although she didn't look any less confused than she had before.

Violet turned back to me. "I think you're mad, Ivy. She won't help you. At best, she might trick you. At worst, she'd *kill* you."

I'd been expecting that. "But she's in prison," I reminded her. "I don't think even Miss Fox would be able to commit a crime *in* prison."

Scarlet twisted her mouth. "Good point. She's not that stupid."

"But she doesn't really have anything left to lose," Violet muttered.

They were missing the point. "She'll be behind bars anyway," I said. "I'm not suggesting we get in with her. We could send a letter..."

My twin shook her head. "She'd just ignore it."

"Or maybe Miss Finch would help us," I tried.

Penny just laughed. "Good luck with that." I glanced over at Nadia, but she was just looking a little annoyed and not saying anything.

The only person who didn't seem to have reacted in any way was Ariadne. I sought out her face among the group, but I couldn't read her expression. "Ariadne?" I tried. "What do you think?"

She bit her lip. "Actually... I think I agree with you."

Scarlet gasped, as did several of the others.

"*Seriously?*" Violet threw her hands up in despair.

"Yes," Ariadne said, giving her an angry glance. "Ivy wouldn't suggest this if it wasn't our only hope, or if she hadn't thought it through. We should trust her."

I felt the cloud of darkness over my head start to lift. Finally, someone understood. *Thank you*, I mouthed.

She nodded and stood up. "I say we do it. Or try, at least. If we don't try, how will we ever know? She could have vital information that would stop Henry and save the school!" She bent down and picked up her paper and pen. "As secretary, I think we need to vote on it."

There were a few nods and words of agreement.

"Okay," I said tentatively.

"All in favour of Ivy trying to question Miss Fox, raise your hand," Ariadne said, putting on her most authoritative voice.

As I put up my own hand, I looked around at the others, praying they would see things my way. Quickly, Ariadne raised her hand as well. And, after a pause, Ebony did too. "Why not?" she said with a shrug.

There was a heavy silence after that. Nobody else moved.

Ariadne sighed and lowered her arm. "All those opposed to the idea, raise your hand."

With a sinking feeling in my heart, I watched three hands

shoot up – Scarlet's, Violet's and even Penny's. Rose looked conflicted, but she obviously understood how Violet felt on the matter – and soon her hand followed her best friend's.

Nadia was the only person who hadn't voted. She shrugged when I looked at her. "I don't care either way," she said. "Maybe it's a good idea. Maybe it isn't."

Ariadne turned to me. "Sorry, Ivy. Four against three, even without Nadia's vote."

I sank down on to the bed. "Then what do we do?" I asked eventually.

Nobody had an answer.

For the next couple of days, we all went around feeling a strange sense of resigned dread. Ariadne had been obliged to return the documents on Rookwood's history to the library before Jing got in trouble with Miss Jones, and we were officially out of ideas.

I didn't resent the others for voting against the idea of talking to Miss Fox – in fact I understood completely. Deep down, I wondered if I'd secretly wanted them to veto it, because I was terrified at the thought of seeing her again. No matter how much anger Scarlet held towards her, no matter how much bravery I'd built up – she was still the person who had beaten us, tried to kill us, locked Scarlet away. As people went, she was rotten to the core. What if I was wrong to hope that she had a shred of decency left in her?

And besides, it was quite likely that my twin was right. Even if we could find some way to contact the ex-headmistress, she probably wouldn't want to help us.

I felt powerless. That night, I dreamt again... but this time I stood in the entrance hall of Rookwood as the building collapsed around my ears, and all I could do was stand still as timbers crashed and girls fell screaming in slow motion into the void below my feet.

Chapter Fourteen

SCARLET

I thought I would feel vindicated by winning the vote, by persuading everyone that we shouldn't talk to Miss Fox. But instead, I felt empty. Now we had nothing to go on.

Each time I saw Henry's smug, smiling, pretty-boy face, I wanted to hit it. He was *still* hanging around the school, him and his inspector. What were they *really* after?

The whole thing left me swimming in a darkly bad mood. And things were about to get worse.

On Fridays, the teachers always did letters in assembly.

That meant they handed out any post that arrived for any of us. Usually, Mrs Knight (or whoever was in charge that day) reading out a short list of names. That day, it was different.

Miss Bowler was up on the stage, facing a huge pile of envelopes on the lectern. There were so many that they were spilling out all across the stage. There were clearly hundreds of the things.

For a moment, she appeared to be speechless, which was unheard of for Miss Bowler.

"Right, you lot!" she shouted at us eventually. "Stop gawping! Everyone has a letter. You'll have to come up one by one and collect it. IN A LINE!"

A younger girl put her hand up. "What are they, Miss?"

Miss Bowler's cheeks puffed out. "No questions! You can read the blasted thing!" She clapped her hands with tremendous force. "Line, now! Quietly!"

It was pretty difficult for the entire school to get in a line without making any noise, but for once we did our best. It was like Miss Bowler was a bomb and we were afraid of setting her off. She was clearly seething on the stage.

By the time we had made it into the queue, it was already snaking all the way round the hall and out of the door. Everyone shuffled forward, necks craning to see the pile of envelopes. I couldn't make out any writing on the outside.

"Pick it up and leave!" Miss Bowler boomed at a girl who was trying to open hers in front of the stage. "You're holding everyone up!"

I shared a quiet look of confusion with Ivy and our friends. What on earth was going on?

It seemed to take forever to get to the front, but when we did, the pile had got considerably smaller. The group of us each grabbed a letter before hurrying out.

The noise everyone had been holding back in the hall grew louder and louder as we left and walked through the corridors. Other teachers were out there, ordering everyone to get to class and read the letters there.

Well, I wasn't about to wait. As soon as we found a place to stand, I ripped mine open.

It read:

Dear Rookwood student and/or parent:

As the owner of the school, I regret to inform you that it is to be closed. The inspector has said the building is in poor repair, and may need to be knocked down. If this is the case, we will be looking into creating a new school building on the site.

Rookwood will likely be closing a few months

before the conclusion of the school year. All students will need to return home and take their belongings with them.

Regrettably, this does of course mean that the school recital will therefore be cancelled.

Regards,
Henry Bartholomew

I balled the letter up in my fist and threw it at the wall. "That twisted snake! I'll kill him!"

I was waiting for Ivy to tell me off, but she was staring in stunned silence at the letter. Ariadne and Ebony were silent too.

To my surprise, Rose was the first one to say something. "I've never got a letter before," she said quietly. "But I'm not sure I wanted this one."

That made me even angrier. Henry had upset Rose, the gentlest person on the planet. He was destroying our school. He didn't even care enough to address us personally. And as if that wasn't enough, he was cancelling the ballet recital. My role as the star of *Swan Lake* – all right, I hadn't won it yet, but I would – just thrown out of the window. It was as though he wanted to personally crush my dreams into the ground and spit on them.

"There's no chance that he'll build a new school," I said, feeling the rage burn in my cheeks. "It's all lies, I'm sure of it. He just wants to destroy the evidence of what Mr Bartholomew did!"

"I-I can't believe it," Ariadne stuttered. "I mean, I knew it was what he wanted to do, but... this is so official, and so soon."

"My father isn't going to like this," Ebony said, frowning.

"What is Henry playing at?" Ivy said finally. She shook her head and folded the letter away into her satchel.

"I think he's playing some sort of twisted game of chess," Ebony said, "and he just knocked all our pieces off the board."

I clenched my fists. "This isn't a game any more. He just declared war."

At lunch, Penny approached the Richmond House table and dropped her tray down beside us. "I'm changing my vote," she said.

I almost spat out my drink. "What? You can't do that."

"I don't see why not," she said. "I'm not having *Barty* order us about like this. I think Ivy was right. We have to know what he's really up to, and Miss Fox might be the only one devious enough to help take him down."

"Ariadne?" I turned to my friend. "Is that in the club rules?"

"Um," Ariadne replied sheepishly, "we don't actually have any rules."

I glared down at the table as I made an angry mental note to write some rules. "Well, I don't see why we should have to change what we voted just because you—"

Nadia appeared behind me. "I want to change my vote too," she said. "I'm with Penny. I trust him about as far as I can throw him. He needs to be stopped before he destroys this place. It is time for a last resort."

I looked at Ivy, dreading seeing a smug expression on her face. But of course, she wasn't like that. She just looked worried. "I don't know..." she said. "You all made good points against it."

"That was Tuesday," Nadia said. "This is today. Things change."

My mouth flapped uselessly. I wasn't expecting this. I felt as though not only had our pieces been knocked off the board, but the table had been flipped upside down too.

"We should ask Violet and Rose," Ivy said. "Or at least let them know if we're going to try it."

"*Try it?*" I stood, my chair scraping on the dining hall floor. "How are you proposing we even attempt this?"

"We talk to Miss Finch," Ivy said, with an annoying slow patience. "I keep telling you."

"Fine." I threw my hands out in exasperation. "You do it. See how well it turns out. I'm going to find Violet and Rose. They'll back me up."

They didn't back me up.

"Maybe Ivy is right," Violet said, making more eye contact with her sandwich than she was with me.

I couldn't believe it. "You've changed your tune!"

Rose said something, but I couldn't hear her over the usual lunchtime din.

Violet sighed. "I don't know. I'm not saying it's a good idea – I still don't think anyone should go within ten feet of her. But with this letter –" she picked it up and waved it at me – "it all feels a bit more real. The school is closing, and it might be forever."

"Not if I can help it," I told her with certainty.

"Then maybe you need to take a risk," she said.

Rose looked up at me with wide eyes, and then just nodded.

I walked off in a huff, heading back to our table. How could everyone have reversed their decisions so quickly? I agreed that the letter had changed things. But not enough that I wanted to walk into what essentially felt like the gaping mouth of a shark. You trusted Miss Fox at your peril.

But then... what if I was right, and Miss Finch wouldn't

even know where her mother was, or refused to speak to her? Then we wouldn't have to do it anyway. As I made my way back through the tables, I began to convince myself. I would go along with what the others wanted, I would be proved correct and it wouldn't get us anywhere. That way, everybody won.

Well, except then we'd still have nothing, and Rookwood would be knocked down. But I was trying to forget that part.

"What's the verdict?" Ivy asked as I returned to my seat.

"We'll do it," I said. "We'll ask Miss Finch after ballet."

Ivy breathed out. "All right."

Ariadne smiled, but her eyes weren't in it.

"For what it's worth," Ebony added, "I think you're doing the right thing."

Now it was my turn for a weak smile. Inside, I was praying that Miss Finch would tell us to take a hike.

Because, deep down, facing Miss Fox again was more frightening than anything else I could imagine.

Chapter Fifteen

IVY

I spent the whole afternoon dreading our ballet lesson. Scarlet kept making sarcastic jokes about how my plan was going to go.

"'So, Miss, you know how your mother was basically a murderer and tried to destroy the school? Do you fancy letting us have a chat with her?'"

Normally I would have laughed and swatted her away, but I was feeling too anxious. What if she was right, and it really was ridiculous... or dangerous?

Descending the stone steps into the ballet studio, I felt even chillier than usual. I rubbed my arms and tried to avoid looking in the mirrors as we crossed the room. We weren't early this time, and several other girls were already warming up, while others sat on the floor lacing on their shoes. We wouldn't have time to talk to Miss Finch until the end of the lesson.

Madame Zelda addressed the class when we were all present. "I'm sure you have all received this... letter," she said derisively. "I don't know what right this man thinks he has to cancel our recital, but—"

"Zelda," Miss Finch interrupted, a warning tone in her voice.

Madame Zelda's eyes went to the stairs as if Henry Bartholomew was about to jump out at her. She sighed. "Well. We will continue our preparation as normal. We will be choosing the roles in two weeks. I trust you will all try your best."

Everyone nodded. "Yes, Miss," we chorused.

She pulled a hairpin from somewhere and stuck it into her tightly wound silver hair. "Now we begin."

I danced my best. When the lesson was finally over, I couldn't catch my breath. I thought it was from effort, but when I began to feel jittery as well I realised it was nerves. I knew what I had to do. Scarlet kept giving me expectant sideways glances.

The trouble was, even as the other girls filtered away, Madame Zelda wasn't leaving. I knew we could trust her, but I didn't think Miss Finch would open up with her around.

But Scarlet had an idea. She grabbed Penny and Nadia before they left. "Can you distract Madame Zelda?" she hissed to them. "Leave us with Miss Finch?"

Penny huffed a bit, but soon nodded her agreement, and Nadia did too.

A few moments later, Nadia had hurled herself to the floor.

"Ouch!" she yelled, grabbing her leg. I think she even managed to squeeze out a few tears. "Miss, I think I twisted my ankle!"

Madame Zelda hurried over, and Miss Finch followed shortly with her cane.

"Get up, Nadia," Madame Zelda said. "We can't have one of our prize dancers out of action."

I couldn't help but notice Miss Finch wincing. Her own accident at the hands of Madame Zelda many years ago had ended her ballet career, and was the reason she still found it hard to walk sometimes.

"It hurts, Miss," Nadia pretend-sobbed.

"All right," Madame Zelda said, sighing. She clicked her fingers at Penny. "Come, Miss Winchester, let's get her to the nurse."

I watched, feeling quietly impressed, as the three of them hobbled away towards the stairs. Nadia had a tendency to be rather dramatic, and this time it had worked in our favour.

"Poor thing," said Miss Finch, biting her lip. She turned to head back to her office.

It's now or never, I told myself.

I shut my eyes for a moment, and let the ballet studio fade away around me. When I opened them again, I tried to pretend I was someone with the courage to do what I had to do.

"Miss Finch," I called out, and trotted across the room, Scarlet following me.

"Yes, Ivy?" the teacher replied, leaning against her piano.

"I... we... wanted to ask you something. It might be a bit of a strange request. I'm sorry..."

Scarlet nudged me in the ribs. I was faltering again. Miss Finch's face remained the same, giving nothing away.

I took a deep breath and tried again. "Do you know where Miss Fox is?"

At that, Miss Finch's mouth dropped open just a little way. She propped her stick against the piano and sat down, rubbing her forehead with one hand. "Yes," she said finally. "She's in Broadgate Prison for..." She gulped and waved her hand. "Everything she did to the school, you know."

"I'm sorry, Miss," I said, "I know it must be hard to talk about—"

"Have you ever been to see her?" Scarlet interjected.

Now Miss Finch looked up sharply. There were some heavy moments of silence during which I was convinced that she was going to say no. But when she opened her mouth again, it was to say, "Yes. Yes, I have." Her cheeks flushed. She was ashamed.

Scarlet shuffled awkwardly and looked away. I knew she would feel betrayed by that after everything Miss Fox had done to her. But just as I'd said, Miss Fox was Miss Finch's real mother, and they'd barely had any time to explore that before our former headmistress had gone on the run and ended up in jail. I could understand. We would do anything for a few minutes with our mother, wouldn't we?

"It's all right, Miss," I tried to reassure her, feeling more than a little uncomfortable.

Miss Finch looked up at me. "Why do you ask?"

I glanced at Scarlet, but she remained tight-lipped. She wasn't going to help me.

"I know this sounds ridiculous, but what with everything that's happened with Henry and him wanting to shut down the school... we wondered if we could talk to her. If... if she might know something. Some important information about Rookwood. That she could tell us." I bit my lip.

An expression of horror grew on our ballet teacher's face as if I'd just told her that I wanted to set myself on fire.

"*What?*" she asked, apparently not believing her ears.

"She's asking if we can talk to her, Miss," Scarlet finally jumped in.

Miss Finch's mouth flapped open. "Girls, I—"

I raced ahead. "You can say no. I know it sounds like an awful idea. But we're not asking this lightly. We've really thought about it. This could be our only chance."

"I'll have to consider this carefully," she said. Her skin had gone even paler than usual. "I'd have to ask Mrs Knight..."

I winced a little at that. Mrs Knight probably wouldn't allow it. But then, Henry infuriated her as much as he did the rest of us. He was taking away her livelihood and throwing us all out in the cold. Perhaps she could be persuaded as well.

"What will happen to you if the school closes for good, Miss?" I asked, my voice almost a whisper.

Our teacher sighed. "I'm afraid things won't go well for me. I only got the job here because of... my mother. It will be very difficult to persuade another school that I can teach dance with my leg being the way it is."

Scarlet muttered a few choice words in Henry's direction, her fists clenched. I felt the same. "You don't deserve this, Miss," she said.

"Thank you, Scarlet," Miss Finch replied. "None of us do. I hoped that Rookwood was becoming a place to be proud of."

"It still could," I told her, and in that moment I really believed it. "If we can just talk to Miss Fox."

Miss Finch put her hand on the piano and lifted herself to her feet. "As I say, I'll think about it. But I'm not promising anything. All right?"

"All right," I said, feeling my heart sinking again. She wasn't saying no yet, but she wasn't saying yes either.

With that, she went into her office and closed the door behind her.

I felt as though the eyes of all of our reflections in the mirrors were staring at me with disappointment. I turned to my twin. "That didn't go *too* badly... did it?" I asked.

Scarlet twisted her mouth and put her hand on my shoulder. "You tried," was all she said.

Chapter Sixteen

SCARLET

I filled the others in about our encounter with Miss Finch at dinner. I didn't know how to feel about it. Of course, it hadn't been a definite *no*, but neither had she been very open to the idea.

But I wanted her to say no.

Didn't I?

The others reacted with varying levels of indifference. There was no real answer for us. We would have to wait, but suddenly I found myself feeling very invested in what Miss Finch would decide. If she said yes, that meant facing the person who was directly responsible for faking my death and trying to ruin my life, not to mention everything else. If she said no, we lost Rookwood, and if my stepmother got her way I could end up right back in the asylum. Needless to say, I didn't like either of those options one bit.

But the next day, things took a turn for the unexpected.

Saturday dawned with an icy chill on the air and a sprinkling of snow. Ivy and I were walking past Mrs Knight's office when the door suddenly opened, and the headmistress shot out, right into our path.

We just about stopped ourselves from colliding with her. "Miss?" I said.

"Girls," she called quietly, her eyes darting round the corridor. "In the office, quick now!"

She hustled us inside and, with another final glance around the hallway, shut the door hurriedly.

"Have I done something wrong?" I asked, since that was usually the reason why I found myself in her office.

The headmistress sat down heavily at her desk. "Sit, please," she said, gesturing to the two chairs in front of it. We sat.

As I looked around her office, I noticed something. All of her pictures with cheerful slogans had been taken down. "What happened to your posters, Miss?"

"He took them," she replied darkly. There were purple bags under her eyes, and her greying hair was sticking up on end. "Because they needed to *inspect the walls*."

"Are you all right, Miss?" Ivy asked. Mrs Knight's expression was a little wild.

After a brisk shake of her head, our headmistress took a deep breath and recomposed herself. "Right. Girls. I've been talking to Miss Finch." She paused. "Of all the stupid, reckless—"

"We're sorry!" Ivy blurted out. "We just thought it might be a good idea to—"

Mrs Knight cut her off with a wave of her hand. "I didn't mean you. I meant me. For what I'm about to do." She blew a lock of hair away from her face. "I give you permission to go and talk to Miss Fox."

I grabbed the desk. "Wait. Are you being serious?"

She nodded, and hesitated a bit before speaking again. "Miss Finch will take you this afternoon."

"Do you..." Ivy started. "Do you think it might work?"

"Girls... You know I have always tried to be cheerful, and to do my best for this school. Well, I find myself in a very sticky situation. Because if I do nothing, the school may be little more than a pile of rubble by next year. And if that happens then none of us will have a job, or a place to learn." Her voice wobbled as she spoke. "If this idea of yours has even the slightest chance of uncovering any information that might help us, then perhaps it's worth a try."

"But Miss Fox... She's so dangerous," I said.

"I know – after all, I worked for Guinevere Fox for many years," Mrs Knight replied. "We were all afraid of her and I never liked her methods. I like to think I have made Rookwood a better place..." There was a filmy sheen over her eyes that she blinked away. "But she knew Rookwood inside out."

I nodded. "She used it against us." Miss Fox had taken advantage of her knowledge of the building to sneak about in the past, when her antics included poisoning the stew and pushing Josephine out of the first-floor window. And she'd known about the hexagonal lodge too, the abandoned house on the edge of the grounds where she'd hidden Miss Finch while terrorising the school.

"I trust Miss Finch to keep you safe," Mrs Knight continued, "but please don't do anything irresponsible." I couldn't help but notice that she was staring at me when she said that.

"We won't," Ivy promised her.

I swallowed. "Are you sure about this, Miss?" I knew I wasn't.

Mrs Knight gripped her desk and stared at nothing for

a moment. "Yes," she said. "Find out anything you can, girls. But please, be careful."

By the afternoon we were waiting in the front hall, bundled up in our coats. I could hear the gentle rustle of the snow falling outside the windows. Ariadne waited with us. "I can't believe it," she kept saying. "I never thought you would get permission."

"I never thought Miss Finch would agree to it," I said miserably. I felt like I was waiting to go to a funeral.

Ivy glanced over at me. She was leaning on the iron radiator. "I'm dreading this too," she said. "It isn't easy for me either."

"I know," I huffed. "So remind me why we're doing it?"

"Because she might tell you something," Ariadne said, with a hint of excitement that I couldn't muster myself. "You could save the school!"

I bit my lip and said nothing.

Shortly, Miss Finch appeared from the corridor. She was walking unaided, slowly but surely.

"Afternoon, Miss," I said. "No stick today?"

She gave me a weak smile. "Well, surprisingly, despite the cold, I'm having a good day. But I imagine it's about to get worse. Come on, before I change my mind."

Help, I mouthed to Ariadne as we left.

Good luck, she mouthed back. Useless!

Mrs Knight had arranged for a motor car to take us; it waited just outside the front doors of the school. I really had to wonder what she had told the driver we were up to, especially since he spent the entire journey staring at us suspiciously in the mirror.

Broadgate Prison was in a village about an hour away from Rookwood. It was an agonising wait as the car bumped through the lanes. My mind alternated between racing, desperately planning what I should say, and a sort of numb denial where I just stared out at the passing hedgerows and tried to pretend we were going somewhere else. Flakes of snow fluttered towards the windscreen like tiny white moths.

Ivy squeezed my hand occasionally. Miss Finch said nothing. I could see her adjusting her scarf and the hem of her dress as she sat in the front seat. Even inside the vehicle, you could see our breath in the air.

Eventually, the car dipped down a small hill, and a number of scattered houses appeared. And then I saw the prison.

First it was just a huge dark shape dusted with white, but it soon became clearer. It was on the left side of the road, and we slowed as we approached it. But you couldn't miss it, really. It was a large Georgian-style building, constructed of solid stone. The tall entrance in the centre had arched windows and an imposing door, while two incredibly high windowless walls stretched out from either side of it.

I felt my heart pound in my chest, and my palms were sweating as I gripped the leather seats. There was no mistaking that this was a prison, and no avoiding what we were here to do.

You could run away, I thought, but I quickly dismissed that as stupid. I had no idea where I was. Where would I go? And besides, Ivy would hate me. She was clearly determined to go through with this ridiculous plan.

As the car came to a halt, the driver helped Miss Finch from the front seat, and Ivy and I clambered out behind her.

"I'll wait," he said shortly, before brushing some snow from his coat and hopping back into the driver's seat.

"Are you sure about this?" I said. I wasn't entirely certain who I was addressing.

"N-no," said Ivy, teeth chattering.

"No," echoed Miss Finch. "Come on. Let's go."

We followed her in through the heavy front door (it took all three of us to pull it open wide enough) and inside the entrance. I felt as though my feet were dragging me along as every fibre of my being protested. I had never felt such an intense urge to *just leave*.

There was a desk across the front of the room, where a tall man in a dark blue prison warden's uniform stood.

"Ma'am," he said, tipping his hat to Miss Finch. "Back to see your mother?"

As we got closer, I saw that despite being tall, he wasn't quite an adult. He had spots, and a strange thing on his upper lip that appeared to be an attempt at a moustache.

"Yes," Miss Finch said. "I hope that's all right?"

He nodded. "And who are these two?" he asked, in an accusing tone.

Ivy's chilly hand gripped mine. I couldn't speak.

Miss Finch, though, didn't seem to struggle for an explanation. "These are my nieces," she lied smoothly, "come to see their grandmother. They miss her terribly."

I watched the disbelief cross the young man's eyes as he tried to imagine Miss Fox being a grandmother, let alone one who anybody missed having around. Nervously, I watched as his hand lingered by the alarm bell on the desk.

But before he could say or do anything, Miss Finch put her hand on his arm. "Thank you, Ronald," she said. I was standing behind her, so I couldn't see, but just the sound of her voice made me think she was fluttering her eyelashes. "I knew you'd understand."

"O-oh," he stammered. "Of course, ma'am. Bertha will show you to the ladies' cells."

Miss Finch turned back to us, her false smile fading. She gave a quick jerk of her head and we followed her off to the side. "This way. I might need some help. The floor's a bit uneven. This place is very old."

"Have a pleasant afternoon, ma'am!" Ronald called after us. His ears had gone red.

"A pleasant afternoon in a prison," I muttered, and Ivy whacked me on the arm.

We helped Miss Finch down the corridor, which did indeed have a bumpy stone floor. At one end, a thickset woman – presumably Bertha – was sitting on a rickety wooden chair. She got to her feet. "Hello again," she said brusquely to Miss Finch, taking her arm from us. She didn't even look at Ivy and me. "Come along."

She took us to another door that looked like it weighed a ton, and pulled from her pocket... a large ring of jangling keys.

My heart went from pounding to racing. I couldn't breathe. "I can't do this," I whispered, but it was loud enough that Ivy heard.

"We can," she said. "We can. Come on."

I watched my twin take a deep breath. She took my hand again.

"Together," she said.

It was time to meet our most terrifying enemy, one last time.

Chapter Seventeen

IVY

We were moments away from meeting Miss Fox. The stone hallway that stretched before us was dark and windowless. It pulled and distorted in front of my eyes. I wondered if we would ever reach the end.

Miss Finch continued with the help of Bertha. If she was as nervous as I thought she must be, she was hiding it well. Beside me, my twin's terror radiated off her. Somehow, it was keeping me strong. One of us had to be. It was strange to think that a few years ago it would never have been me.

We reached another door, and again Bertha stopped to unlock it with a key that looked as old as the building. And as she opened it, I heard the noise.

It wasn't a constant babble of noise like you'd hear in the Rookwood dining hall. It was ebbing and flowing. I could hear machines, someone quietly crying, and then a loud shout, and a clanking sound like someone was running something metal along the bars.

"Settle down, ladies," Bertha called through the doorway. She beckoned us forward. Scarlet's hand was gripping mine so tightly that it had gone white.

We walked in. There were cells on either side of us, black iron bars rising to the ceiling. Each cell looked simple, with wooden slats for a bed, a washbasin, and not much else. The whitewashed stone gave way to a window at the end of each cell, which of course had more bars across it. The room didn't smell unclean so much as old and forgotten.

Some of the women were doing work – weaving on machines, darning clothes. That explained some of what I'd heard.

"Please!" a voice shouted right beside my ear, making me jump. I turned to see a desperate round face pressed to the bars. "I ain't done nothing, I swear!"

Bertha shooed her back. "Hush, Perkins. None of that."

"Well, it's true!" the woman protested, stumbling back.

"I'm innocent too," another woman called from the other side. She was dark, thin and frail, perching on her wooden bed.

I could hear Scarlet's panicked breath, and I realised she was probably reliving her time in the asylum. "It's okay," I whispered to her.

Bertha turned to the thin woman. "Sally the Ripper told me she was innocent every day. Do you think we should have let her out, eh?" She shook her head in disbelief.

I felt a deep sadness in the pit of my stomach. Did all these women really deserve this? How many of them had really been wrongly imprisoned, just like Scarlet? And how many were... well... like Miss Fox?

Despite the sadness, I was also starting to feel numb. Was this really happening?

We reached the end of the row and went through another door. There were small corridors leading off it, with only a few cells. Bertha led us round a dark corner. "Fox!" she bellowed. She reminded me of Miss Bowler, I realised. "Visitors!" She turned back to us. "I'll leave you to it. You have ten minutes." She marched away.

Scarlet caught her breath. I felt my head spin.

We were facing a cell, much like the others, with iron bars and white walls. And there, dressed all in black, leaning against the rear wall with her arms folded... was Miss Fox.

She lifted her head slowly. Her hair was still in its tight bun, pulling her face back. "Ah, Rebecca," she said, in the manner of someone greeting a guest in their parlour, not a prison.

But then she noticed us, standing stock still behind her daughter.

"What. Are they. Doing here?" she growled.

"Mother," Miss Finch said. I expected her to be as scared as we were, but I supposed she'd done this a few times. She just sounded tired. "The twins need to talk to you."

Miss Fox seethed at us, her upper lip quivering in disgust. "You think I would talk to those brats?" she growled. "When all of this was their fault?" She gestured at the cell around her.

"Come on," Miss Finch said, leaning against the wall beside the bars in a mirror of her mother's position. "After all you've done to them, don't you think this is the least you could do?"

I admired our teacher's courage. She had come a long way when it came to standing up to her mother.

Miss Fox put her nose in the air. I could almost feel her stare crawling over my skin. "Did you find out what happened to Raven?" she asked suddenly.

Miss Finch looked exasperated. "I told you, Mother, they found your horse. He's back in the stables at Rookwood. Don't change the subject."

"What subject?" Miss Fox said, still glaring.

Suddenly, Scarlet let go of my hand. The intensity of her grip fell away and all the blood rushed back to my fingertips. She stepped forward. "Look," she said, standing there as if she were facing down a cannon. "We're here to talk to you about something important. Mr Bartholomew is dead. His slimy son has taken over, and if you don't help us, he's probably going to turn Rookwood into a pile of dust in a few weeks. Whatever you think of us, I'm sure that's not what you want."

Now our former headmistress raised an eyebrow. I could tell that what Scarlet had said had piqued her interest. "Is this true, Rebecca?"

"Yes, Mother," Miss Finch told her. "He wants to tear the place down. He says he'll rebuild the school, but we're not very convinced... All of us could be out of a job. I don't think I'll find anywhere else that would take me."

Slowly, Miss Fox sat down on the wooden bed. "That old fool," she muttered. "I knew he'd do this. After everything I built for that place—"

"But you tried to destroy it!" I interrupted.

She shot her glance back over to me. "Exactly. If anyone's going to destroy Rookwood, it's going to be me."

"Mother..." Miss Finch warned. "You're in prison."

"As if I don't know that!" Miss Fox shouted. Scarlet

flinched. "The fact remains, it's my legacy. It's my choice or no one's. It's not for some *man* to come along and throw it all away."

I gave my twin a meaningful look. Miss Fox seemed a little delusional, but I could tell we were getting somewhere.

"We can stop him," Scarlet said, her voice shaking. "You can finally get revenge on Mr Bartholomew. Isn't that what you've always wanted?"

Miss Fox got up again and stalked towards the bars. It unnerved me how quietly she moved now. No clacking heels, no jangling keys. We stayed frozen to the spot, not wanting to get any closer. She glared at us through the bars. "You're children!" she snapped. "What do you know about what I want?"

"We know he treated you terribly," I said, keeping my voice quiet. I was afraid that speaking louder would set her off. "You were afraid of him."

"Pah," she spat, but I could tell her heart wasn't in it.

"You were," I said. Miss Finch nodded. She knew it was true too. "You hated him. And now his horrible son is going to decide everything for us," I reiterated. "Unless you tell us something we can use."

After a few moments of silence, Miss Fox looked away from us, running her fingers along the bars. "He never really owned the school," she said eventually. I took a sharp breath in. *Confirmation!* "I knew that. But do you really think that if I had a way to prove it, that if there was some way I could've taken it from him... that I wouldn't have done it myself?"

I felt my meagre hopes crumbling. But we couldn't give up yet. Not after all this. "Please," I said. "Don't you have any ideas?"

"Hmm." She still didn't want to meet our eyes. I think she didn't even want to admit to herself that she was talking to us. But I had struck a nerve. "There was a suspicion I had..." She tapped her long nails on the bars. The sound set my teeth on edge. "You know of Lady Wootton?"

We nodded.

"My guess was that he'd changed her will, forged the documents. But an old battle-axe like her... I don't think she would've kept only one copy. I thought there was a good chance that she had hidden one somewhere in the building. Perhaps there are secret places yet to be discovered that could contain her real will."

"Where could it be?" I asked.

Miss Fox glanced up again as if she was suddenly back in the room. "Foolish child. I would have found it if I knew!" She tapped her chest. "*I* know every inch of Rookwood. *I* had the key to every room. *I* built that school up from nothing!"

"And look where it got you!" Scarlet responded. I could see a fire burning in her cheeks. Her anger had finally beaten her fear. "Don't forget which side of the bars you're on!"

Miss Finch raised her eyebrows, but she still said nothing.

Miss Fox fixed my twin with an intense stare. "And don't you forget what I can do, even from here," she said in a low voice. "Isn't it funny how easily people can be bribed to forget about you?"

Scarlet's mouth dropped open. "HOW DARE YOU—" she started, moving forward, but I grabbed her and held her back.

"Don't," I whispered. But inside, I felt the same way. So Miss Fox *had* bribed our stepmother, just as we'd always suspected.

"Mother," Miss Finch said again. "I can get Bertha to come back here if you're going to start making threats."

Miss Fox huffed and folded her arms once more. Scarlet panted with anger beside me, her teeth gritted.

I had to speak up. "We won't ever forget what you did," I told her, trying to keep my voice steady. "We had a *funeral* for Scarlet. I'll remember that until the day I die. That's before we even get to all the other unspeakable things you've done. But I'll also remember that we were the ones who stopped you."

Scarlet lifted her chin high and matched our old

headmistress's stare. "The outside world is a better place without you," she said. "It's moving on. We don't need to bribe anyone to forget you. They will anyway."

Miss Finch bit her lip and stared at the floor. She didn't disagree.

"What they will remember," Scarlet said, a fire in her eyes, "is how we saved Rookwood School."

Chapter Eighteen

SCARLET

Miss Fox wouldn't say anything else after that. She was still seething silently as Miss Finch led us away.

"Goodbye, Mother," Miss Finch said. I wondered if it would be for the final time. Somehow, I doubted it. Miss Finch's relationship with her mother was the definition of complicated.

It was only after we had met up with Bertha and made it back to the entrance that I realised I was shaking, and it wasn't from the cold. But now it wasn't from fear either.

Something was rising inside me. A new determination. As Ronald on the front desk chatted to Miss Finch (something that he seemed far more interested in than she did), I turned to Ivy. "We did it," I said. "We actually did it."

She nodded. "If we can talk to Miss Fox, we can do anything."

We didn't speak again for the entire journey back to Rookwood, through the snowy winding lanes. Somehow, words weren't enough.

When we reached the school, we thanked the driver and hopped out. He helped Miss Finch from the front passenger side.

"Well, girls," she said, "I don't know if that was any use to you."

Hmm. I wasn't sure exactly what we had yet, but I thought we might have learnt something important. It was bubbling away inside my mind. "Sorry, Miss," I replied. "I know it's hard."

She squeezed my shoulder. "Sometimes hard things are worth doing."

Inside the foyer, Miss Finch left us (presumably to let Mrs Knight know that we hadn't been murdered or converted to a life of crime), but we found Ariadne and Ebony waiting for us. We walked towards them, our footsteps echoing across the floor.

Ariadne jumped up with surprising energy. "Scarlet! Ivy! What happened?"

Even Ebony seemed more interested than usual. "Tell us everything," she said. I gave her a suspicious look, and she shrugged in response. "Ariadne's been working me up about this the whole time you've been gone."

I chuckled, and Ariadne gave an embarrassed smile.

"Well—" Ivy started.

"It was awful," I interrupted. "Really awful. And I never, ever, want to go there again."

"Oh no," said Ariadne, her face falling. Ebony looked sympathetic.

"*But,*" Ivy said, "we learnt something. According to Miss Fox, Mr Bartholomew *did* steal the school from Lady Wootton, and he changed her will. And her theory is that the original document is still here in the school."

Ebony gasped. "Which would prove that Henry isn't the real owner!"

"Exactly." I nodded. "There's a catch, though. Miss Fox didn't have a clue where it might be hidden, or if she did, she wasn't saying. But honestly, I think she was telling the truth. She would have found it if she'd known, and used it to steal the school herself. She's familiar with every inch of this place."

Ariadne looked ponderous. "So if the will really exists, that leaves two choices – either it's in a place so secret that even Miss Fox couldn't find it, or it's hidden in plain sight."

Hmm. That was a good point. And neither of those options were particularly promising for us.

"There's more," Ivy told them. "She also more or less admitted that our stepmother accepted a bribe from her to pretend Scarlet was dead."

Ariadne slapped her hands over her mouth.

"Wait, what?" Ebony asked.

"Long story," I said.

In the early evening, I called a meeting of the new Whispers in our room again to explain what we had learnt. We pulled the curtains shut to try to keep some of the warmth in.

Penny wrinkled her nose as soon as I'd finished speaking. "Is—"

I pointed at her. "I know what you're going to say, so save it. *Is any of that useful?* Well, I think it *was* worth it." *It has to be*, I thought.

"Hmmph," Penny snorted. "And here was me thinking you were dead against the idea."

"I was," I said, shooting her a glare. "That was then. This is now."

"The *real* question," said Ivy, in a not-so-subtle hint that she wanted us to stop arguing, "is what are we going to do with this information?"

Ariadne raised her hand. "I think we need to go back to the drawing board, and look over everything we know—"

"Or," Nadia interrupted, "we just start searching right away. We don't have much time."

"And search the entire school?" I asked. "Where exactly do you propose we start? And besides, Henry and his henchman seemed to have searched the entire school already. Well, perhaps not our dorms, but everywhere else."

"We need something to go on," Ariadne agreed, scribbling a few words on her notepad. "But we *do* have a clue. We know that there probably is a will belonging to Lady Wootton, and that she might have hidden it somewhere in the school. So we just have to think like her."

Penny threw her hands up in the air. "Think like some old dead woman. Of course! Why didn't that occur to me? Simple!"

"Penny," I said flatly. "Do you want to be part of this group or not?"

She responded with some angry grumbling, but she didn't argue further.

"Right." I stood up. "Meeting adjourned. Try to... have good ideas." I waved at them to leave.

Ariadne nodded at Ebony. "We'll work on it."

"See you at dinner," Ivy said to them.

Once they'd all left, I threw myself face down on my bed. I'd really had enough. Why did everything have to be so difficult?

Ivy poked me in the arm. "Come on. Don't give up."

"Go away," I mumbled into the pillow. "I'm asleep."

"It's been three seconds," she said. "And we should be thinking about this too."

I rolled on to my side. "I'm just exhausted with all of them at the moment. With all of this, all of today. I can't believe we talked to Miss Fox!"

Ivy nodded and stared out of the window. "It was... draining."

Now we sat in silence. I noticed something, though. I felt... *different*. A little lighter. As if seeing Miss Fox in prison, and confronting her, had relieved me of a weight I hadn't known I was carrying. I didn't feel that horrible dread when I said her name any more.

Perhaps going through all of that *had* been worth it. Even if the information didn't lead us anywhere, we'd still gained something.

We'd gone head to head with Miss Fox – and won.

I was woken on Sunday morning by someone shaking me. "Ugh," I moaned. "Ivy, stop it."

"Not Ivy! It's Ariadne! Wake up, both of you!"

I cracked one eye open sleepily to see our friend standing beside our beds in her nightgown, her hair frizzy and unbrushed. She was clutching her notebook.

"What?" I exclaimed. "What's going on? How did you get in here?"

"I just walked in," she said. "Sorry. But it's important!"

Ivy's head appeared from under her bedsheets. "W-what?"

"You said to have good ideas. Well, I think I've had one!"

That got my attention. I sat up quickly and pushed the covers aside. "Come on, then, tell us!"

Ariadne plonked herself down on the foot of my bed. "All right. We need to find where Lady Wootton might have hidden her will. So where would you hide something important?"

"In my mattress," I said without hesitation.

"In a wardrobe?" Ivy suggested.

Ariadne nodded. "You're thinking along the right lines. I think it's quite likely that she would hide it in her bedroom, especially if that was the only part of Rookwood that was really hers in the end. But if it was in any of her furniture, presumably old Mr Bartholomew would have found it."

I thought about it. "She could have had some secret place in there that he had no idea about. Under the floorboards, maybe. In the ceiling."

"Exactly," Ariadne agreed. "So we need to get in there."

Ivy shuffled herself upright on her pillows. "Wait," she said. "Wasn't her bedroom where Matron's apartment is now?"

"Yes," Ariadne replied, looking down at her notebook. "According to the initials on the map."

I screwed up my face. "Well, that's not good. How on earth are we going to get in there?"

"How indeed," Ivy said. "She's in there all the time."

Ariadne flattened her notebook out on my bed. "That's where my plan comes in." She took a deep breath. "Remember the dumbwaiter?"

Ivy went a bit white. "Oh no, not again..."

Chapter Nineteen

IVY

Scarlet looked confused by Ariadne's suggestion of the dumbwaiter. "You mean the cupboard things that go down to the basement?"

I stared at her. "Don't you remember – you made me get in it! To find your diary entry! It was horrible!"

"Oh, it wasn't that bad," she scoffed.

I threw a pillow at her head. "How can you say that? You're claustrophobic and afraid of the dark!"

"Only recently... I didn't mind at the time!"

"Anyway," Ariadne continued pointedly, "the thing is, it doesn't just go down. It goes up too. It was used to send meals upstairs from the kitchen."

Scarlet emerged from under the pillow. "But I've never seen it up here."

Ariadne grinned at her. "Exactly! That's because the original corridor it was in got built into Matron's apartment! It was marked with a little square on the map. I couldn't figure out what it was until I saw that it lined up on every floor."

I really didn't like the idea of getting back in that dumbwaiter again. It was a dreadful creaking box of darkness. "Would we all have to get in it?" I asked nervously.

"We wouldn't fit," Scarlet teased.

"One at a time, I mean," I said. "And would we have to break into the kitchen again to get into it in the first place?"

Ariadne turned back to me. "Well, let me explain. I think this plan is going to take all of us." She pulled a piece of paper out of her notebook, with a complicated-looking diagram scribbled on it.

"Did you do all that this morning?" Scarlet asked in dismay.

Ariadne waved the paper at her. There was a slightly wild look in her eyes. "All night! Now look." She smoothed it out on the bed. "This dumbwaiter goes all the way to the top floor – above Matron's apartment. We need someone stationed there to pull it up and down. Then we need someone to cause a distraction, to get Matron out of her room for as long as possible. But the problem is she's had a latch put on her door, so it locks when she leaves the room." Ariadne pulled out a pencil from behind her ear and pointed at a little stick figure with curly hair and MATRON written on her dress. "So while she's distracted, one person needs to get in the dumbwaiter and get pulled down into the apartment. They can then unlock the door from the inside, and the rest of us can go in and search."

Scarlet looked impressed, if a little confused, as she stared at the diagram. "That's genius."

"As long as we don't get caught..." I said. Then a thought floated to the front of my sleepy mind. "Wait a minute. Why don't we just ask Matron if we can search her room?"

"I just did," said Ariadne.

We both looked at her. "What?"

Ariadne shrugged. "I just knocked on her door and asked her. I told her it was terribly important, and that it would surely save the school."

"And what did she say?" I asked.

Ariadne put on her best impersonation of Matron. "'*Over my dead body. Go back to bed, Flitworth, it's seven o'clock in the morning on a Sunday.*'"

Scarlet nodded with appreciation. "Great impression. You could almost hear the hair curlers and the dressing gown. And besides, if Henry hears that we've been poking around in there, it'll tip him off. We should keep this secret."

"Right," I said. I threw the covers off my bed. I was well and truly awake at this point, so I thought it would be best to make the most of it. "So what do we do now?"

Ariadne grinned.

My twin had a devious look in her eye. "We assemble the Whispers," she said.

At breakfast, Scarlet rounded up the whole group and told them to come to our room afterwards. Once we were all together, Ariadne explained the plan.

There were some arguments (no one will be surprised to hear that these were mostly from Penny) but eventually we had a list of roles assigned to each person.

1. *Ebony, Violet and Nadia - create a distraction*

2. *Penny - winching the dumbwaiter*

3. *Rose - lookout*

164

4. Scarlet - riding in the dumbwaiter

5. Ivy and Ariadne - searching the
room

This had been decided on the basis that Ebony, Violet and Nadia all excelled at being dramatic, and that they would come up with a good distraction. They were currently whispering ideas to each other and cackling. Penny thought the whole thing was probably a waste of time, but we'd talked her into operating the dumbwaiter and she was at least mildly interested as she'd never used one before.

Rose, as the quietest and most observant of us all, was the ideal candidate to keep a lookout outside Matron's room. We'd decided that it wasn't necessary to station anyone on the top floor, since no one ever went up there except for spiders and, well, us, when we were searching for secrets.

I had flat-out refused to go in the dumbwaiter again, but had managed to convince Scarlet to give it a go. Perhaps facing her fears would be good for her. She kept insisting she wasn't afraid, but I didn't really believe her.

That left Ariadne and me to join her in searching Matron's apartment. Honestly, more than being caught, my biggest fear was that we would find nothing.

"We'll wait until eight o'clock this evening," Scarlet said, "when everyone's in their rooms. Then we'll put the plan into action."

There were nods of agreement.

I crossed my fingers tightly. If this went well and we found something... we could change everything.

Evening came. We had to avoid talking about the plan over dinner, in case someone heard us. Scarlet kept winking at the others.

Sunday evenings were always one of the quietest times at Rookwood. Most people retreated to their rooms, having eaten too much stew or forgotten to do their prep work for Monday. We'd been sensible and finished ours earlier in the day (or at least I had – Scarlet claimed that she'd done hers, but it had looked an awful lot like writing in her diary and eating sweets she'd stolen from Ariadne). There were only a few people about in the corridor, heading to the bathrooms or gossiping by their dorms.

I heard the distant chime of the clock striking eight. It was time to go.

Scarlet and I sneaked out of our room, and found Ariadne waiting just outside. I could see Rose walking down the corridor towards Matron's apartment. We followed her, trying to look casual. She was to give us a signal once Matron had left.

As we passed Nadia's room, Nadia, Violet and Ebony spilt out into the hallway.

Nadia winked at us, took a deep breath, and yelled, "HOW DARE YOU?"

Violet gave her a theatrical shove. "I DON'T HAVE TO EXPLAIN MYSELF TO YOU!"

"Stop, just stop!" Ebony cried at them.

They continued shouting at each other. Curious faces peered out from doors.

"You're such a…" Nadia started, before saying an insult so nasty it made Ariadne blush, and gasps echoed along the hallway.

"You take that back, you vile slug!" Violet said with just the right amount of feigned disgust. It was strange to see her acting this way. This was more like the Violet that Scarlet had written about in her diary, the one who bossed everyone around and attacked people. Violet had changed so much after her experiences in the asylum, and her friendship with Rose.

Speaking of Rose, I caught sight of her waving frantically from the other end of the corridor. Matron was coming!

This time, Nadia shoved Violet, who fell back against the door.

"Fight! Fight!" some of the nearby nosy girls started chanting.

Making the best of the distraction, we scurried for the stairs and began jogging up to the third floor.

"Girls?" I heard Matron's voice calling, and the sound of her footsteps pounding as she broke into a run. "Girls! Stop this *immediately*!"

At that point I heard Ebony give her best, most bloodcurdling scream.

Penny was waiting at the top of the stairs, leaning against a wall. "What on earth are they doing?"

"I don't know," Ariadne said, "but it's working!"

"It's certainly distracting," I acknowledged, "but I'm not sure what we'll do if they all get expelled."

"No time to worry about that," Scarlet said. If I had to guess, I would have said she wasn't that bothered by the prospect anyway. "Come on." She waved at us to follow her, and we all hurried along towards the dumbwaiter.

"I've pulled the thing up already," Penny told us. "I thought they might still be using it in the kitchen, but I think they've all gone home. At least, nobody stopped me, and it's empty." She gestured towards the contraption.

The dumbwaiter looked like a cupboard set into the wall of the empty and echoey third floor. Usually the doors that covered it would be left shut, but now it was wide open, like a gaping mouth just waiting to devour one of us.

Scarlet gulped. "Is it too late to change my mind?"

"Yes," I said, giving her a gentle shove forward. "There's no time. We've only got as long as the others can keep Matron away from her apartment for."

"Right. Right." Scarlet ran a hand through her hair and exhaled a nervous breath. "Okay."

"You can do it!" Ariadne cheered her on.

"*Okay!*" Scarlet retorted. "I'm going!"

Ariadne turned to me. "We need to get back downstairs. Come on, there's a staircase this way!"

Chapter Twenty

SCARLET

I hesitated before the dark void of the open dumbwaiter. Penny was glaring at me. "What are you waiting for?" she asked. "This was your lot's genius plan, so you can blooming well get on with it." She gave me a gentle shove, which from Penny was about the closest you would get to a hug.

I reached forward and pulled myself up into it. I had to curl tightly into a ball, and I couldn't turn round. Hadn't Ivy managed this more easily last year? We must have grown.

"Here we go," I heard Penny's voice say from behind me. I heard a whirring, creaking sound as she began winching and the dark cupboard lurched downwards.

I breathed slowly, in and out. *It's fine*, I told myself. *Small, dark spaces can't hurt you.*

There was a strange, sick feeling in my stomach, like I was falling slowly. I tried very, very hard not to move. I had a sudden fear that my hair might get caught or I'd fall backwards and get scraped along the wall. I clutched my legs more tightly. The noise grated against my ears.

Eventually, I felt some fresh (or at least slightly fresher) air on my back, and everything got lighter.

And then there was a jolt, and the thing stopped. Cautiously, I reached behind me, and couldn't feel a wall. Instead I felt something like fabric.

I tried to climb out, but I was stuck. My limbs were folded at awkward angles. There was only one thing for it, and it wasn't going to be very graceful. So I took a deep breath, and tipped myself out backwards.

I landed heavily on the carpet with a *thud*.

As I stared up at the ceiling, my head spinning, I realised that the dumbwaiter had been covered with a curtain on this level instead of the wooden doors it had up above. And thank goodness for that, because it was only just now occurring to me that I could have been trapped in there.

I climbed to my feet and turned to look around. I was in a small corridor within Matron's suite of rooms with nothing much in it, save for a plant and a wooden chest. I ventured out cautiously, but there was no sign of Matron. Of course, if she had been there, she probably would've noticed when a girl fell out of her wall.

Matron's living room was large with bright, airy windows and framed paintings all over the patterned wallpaper. It was full of comfortable-looking wooden furniture, draped with blankets. A wireless sat on a table in the centre surrounded by magazines, and a pair of knitting needles with some half-finished pink knitting had been set down beside it.

Through an archway I glimpsed a kitchen that looked fairly tidy, with a dresser full of pink and white china. Through another archway I could see Matron's bedroom, containing a cosy double bed covered with quilts – far nicer than our lumpy singles.

But before I could investigate any further, I heard a soft knock on the door.

Ivy and Ariadne! That was the signal. I had to let them in.

I looked around to get my bearings and found the door that I hoped must lead out to the corridor. I ran over, twisted the latch and pulled it open... and there were Ivy and Ariadne on the other side.

"You did it!" Ariadne grinned.

"Quick, quick," I whispered, ushering them in and peering over their shoulders as I did so. I could see Rose playing lookout – she gave me a small wave. And I could still hear the commotion from down the corridor. The distraction was working wonders, but we had no way of knowing just how long we would get to search. I pulled the door shut behind them.

"Let's split up," Ivy said as she took in the apartment. "I'll go in the kitchen; Ariadne can go in the bedroom; Scarlet – you look around the living room. If one of us finishes we'll come out and search with you."

"Okay," I said, rubbing my hands together. Ariadne nodded and ran off towards the bedroom.

Where do I start?

I looked down at the floor. There were floorboards, but mostly they were covered with threadbare carpets and rugs. I paced the room, trying to feel with my feet if any of the boards were loose, if they could have something hidden underneath. But nothing shifted – they were solid.

"Matron has a *lot* of tea," Ivy called from the kitchen.

"Oh no," I heard Ariadne say. "There are *underthings* in here..."

I ignored them. I had to concentrate. Where else to look? *Furniture?* There were chairs and bureaux and a desk, but I thought it was quite unlikely that they had been there since Lady Wootton's time. They looked newer. And besides, unless they had a very well-hidden secret compartment, wouldn't Matron have found anything hidden in them by now?

Walls, then. I went back to the door and began to feel my way along the wall. "Don't forget to check under the paintings!" I called to the others. Every time I reached a painting, I lifted the frame and peered underneath it. One was so high up that I had to grab a stool and stand on it. The smooth golden frame unleashed a cloud of dust into my face, and I sneezed.

"Bless you," Ivy said, emerging from the kitchen. "I can't find anything out of the ordinary."

But then... "I think I've got something," came Ariadne's voice. "Help?"

We rushed into the bedroom to find her struggling with a heavy painting of a woman.

"I think... there's... something underneath!" she said, her words straining.

Ivy and I grabbed the opposite corner and took the weight, and together the three of us lifted the painting off the wall and laid it carefully on the floor.

There was a small door, halfway up the wall. The wallpaper was bright and colourful in a square round it, where the painting had kept the light off for many years. The door itself was flat and painted white, with a small handle.

Ariadne's eyes went from the door to the painting and back again. "I thought the painting might be of Lady Wootton," she said. The woman in the picture certainly looked like a Lady. She was young and draped in jewels, with a sharp expression in her dark eyes.

"I think you might be right," Ivy said. She bent down and wiped a thick layer of dust from the bottom of the frame, and the initials EMW appeared – just like on the map.

We all stood there in silence for a moment, just staring at the door.

"Come on," I said finally. "We need to open it!" But I knew why they were hesitating. At that moment, that door contained infinite potential. It could be hiding just what we needed to save the school. But if we opened it and there was nothing there? Our dreams could be dashed.

"You do it," Ivy said. "You're closest." Ariadne said nothing.

"All right," I snapped. "Fine." But I still took another moment to stare at it. I could feel the portrait's eyes on me as if Lady Wootton was saying, *"Go on, I dare you..."*

Ivy prodded me in the arm.

"Wait," I said. "What if it's a trap?"

Ivy and Ariadne both fixed me with confused expressions. "What?"

I shuffled my feet on the rug. "Well, I mean, she was crafty. What if she wanted to keep Mr Bartholomew from taking her real will? We could open this and a poison arrow could shoot out. Or a thousand spiders." I was sure I'd seen that at the pictures once.

"That's not going to happen," Ivy said, but she'd gone a little pale.

"Let's *all* open it," Ariadne said finally. "Okay?"

We nodded at each other. "Okay."

With some difficulty, we all took hold of the handle and inhaled deeply.

"One... two... three!"

We pulled, and the door sprang open to reveal...

A solid, iron safe, with a combination dial and three keyholes.

And not a key in sight.

Chapter Twenty-one

IVY

We stared at the sturdy safe in silence. All of that work, and we were faced with a locked box!

After a few moments, I stepped forward and tried pulling on the door, in the vain hope that it might budge. It didn't even slightly wobble.

Ariadne pulled one of her trusty hairpins from her pocket. "I don't know if I can pick these," she said. "They look pretty solid."

"And even if you could," Scarlet pointed out, "there's a dial as well. We need to find the combination."

But just as Ariadne was about to try it, Rose came running into the room, panting.

"Matron is coming back," she said in a loud whisper (which was more like a scream, coming from Rose).

We all looked at each other.

"Quick!" Ariadne squeaked.

She slammed the wooden cover back over the safe and together we lifted the heavy painting back up. Then all of us ran out of the apartment, footsteps slamming against the floor, the front door swinging shut behind us.

"There's no time to escape," I hissed, knowing that Matron would see us running, which would no doubt look worse. "We have to do something!"

Rose contemplated this for a tiny amount of time before putting her hand to her head and dramatically swooning to the floor.

Seconds later, Matron appeared. "What on earth...?" she started, seeing us crowded around her door.

"Oh, Miss!" Scarlet exclaimed. Her face was flushed. "Rose was just getting so worried about Violet and the others fighting that she's fainted!"

That was quick thinking. Ariadne and I nodded in pretend agreement.

Rose, hearing her cue, put her hand on her head and sat up again, groaning.

"For goodness' sake, girls," Matron said. "I've only just sorted out that lot! Don't you start! Are you all right, Rose?"

She didn't seem to notice anything out of the ordinary. This was good.

Rose made a great effort of clambering to her feet. "Yes, Miss," she whispered. "I'll be fine."

"Good," Matron snapped. "Rose, go and lie down until you feel better. Now, the rest of you, get back to your dorms and stay out of trouble. I need a cup of tea."

She pushed past us, unlocked her apartment and went inside, leaving us in the corridor.

As we were walking away as innocently as possible, I heard a distant exclamation from inside Matron's room.

"WHO MOVED MY KNICKERS?"

"Run!" Scarlet said.

We hid in our room for the rest of the evening, with Penny joining us. Just before lights-out, there was a soft knock on our door and Violet, Nadia and Ebony came slinking in.

"We all got detention," Nadia said. "For a week. And we have to write essays on why fighting is wrong." She rolled her eyes.

"Please tell me the plan worked," Ebony said, sitting down heavily on the floor. "I quite enjoyed the fighting, but now we've just spent an hour listening to Mrs Knight explaining the power of friendship and positive thinking."

Violet nodded. "It better have been worth it."

I looked at Scarlet. "Well... yes and no."

The three of them visibly deflated. Rose went over and put her arm round Violet.

"Don't get disheartened just yet," I said. "Let us explain."

"I'm all ears," said Nadia, flinging her arms out.

Scarlet told them what we'd found – the painting of Lady Wootton, the mysterious locked safe beneath.

Ebony's eyes had lit up. "You don't go to that much trouble to lock something up if it isn't important," she said. "There's a safe like that at the theatre where they keep all the takings and the deeds. They have several keys so that if one person wanted to steal all the valuables, they wouldn't be able to. Even with one key and combination, they have to get the keys from the other two."

"Exactly," Ariadne said. "But the question is, how do we find the combination?"

"And where did the keys go?" I finished.

Nobody had any suggestions. We were all stumped.

This could just be the first mystery to leave us completely in the dark. And if we couldn't come up with something soon, Rookwood, as we knew it, was finished.

*

I spent the night tossing and turning. Every time I was about to fall asleep, the safe sprang into my mind, and I would start worrying about it again. But I still didn't have any idea how we could get into it.

As Monday dawned with cold, white light through our bedroom window, I was feeling more positive. But it didn't last long.

After the traditional Rookwood porridge breakfast, we walked into morning assembly to a cacophony of sound. Straight away, I noticed that Henry was standing on the stage, with his inspector. He was wearing yet another fancy tailored suit.

Everyone was talking and shouting. Henry looked mildly annoyed, tapping his spotless shoes and looking at his pocket watch.

"Why are you doing this?" I heard someone say as we pushed our way to our seats.

"This is ridiculous!"

"It isn't fair!"

"Save our school!"

Mrs Knight was at the front of the hall, and I could see she was trying to calm people down, but you couldn't hear her over the din. Was Miss Bowler not there? I looked around – but no, Miss Bowler was just standing on the other side of the hall. She had her arms folded, and a smug expression on her face. *She's rather enjoying this*, I thought.

I glanced at Scarlet and Ariadne, who both just shrugged. We would have to wait to find out what was going on now.

Eventually, Miss Bowler got fed up with waiting. "RIGHT! SHUT UP, YOU LOT!"

Some people quietened down, but there were still shouts. That was surprising – usually you got dead silence when Miss Bowler yelled.

"I MEAN IT!" her voice boomed across the hall. "QUIET, NOW!"

The sound of angry voices faded away to a trickle, and then to nothing.

"*Thank* you," said Henry. "Now—"

"I didn't do it for you," Miss Bowler said, before turning on her heel and walking out.

Ha! I thought.

Henry frowned and sniffed. Then he adjusted his suit – and it was as if his face reset, back into his usual smile. "Now, girls. I hope you all received my letters. Well, I have something to let you know."

My heart sank. Not more revelations, surely?

"Next week, the school will be closing down for further inspections and works. We need all pupils and teachers to return home for the entire seven days."

"*What?*" someone exclaimed, opening the floodgates to another rush of noise. The inspector winced.

Henry waved his arms until everyone went quiet again. "There are no exceptions. The school must be empty. It's very dangerous work." He glanced at his watch again. "Anyway," he said, giving his winning smile, "I must be going."

With that, he marched out, his inspector trotting behind him. And once again, the hall erupted into shouts and conversation.

"Liar!" Scarlet yelled, jumping to her feet. "He's lying!"

I shushed her and pulled her back down.

"He is!" she insisted. She lowered her voice and hissed, "Do you think he wants to find the safe?"

"Well, I don't think he knows what he's looking for," I said.

Ariadne leant over. "Even if he finds it, he won't be any better off than us."

She had a point. He wouldn't have the keys or the combination either.

"Ugh," Scarlet moaned. "He's vile."

I sat back in my seat as the commotion flowed around the hall. I had just realised exactly what Henry's announcement most likely meant for us, and it was something even more vile.

Another week with our stepmother.

Chapter Twenty-two

SCARLET

Every time we passed Mrs Knight's office for the next few days, she was either frantically scribbling letters or on the telephone saying, "I know it's last minute, but I'm afraid our hands are tied!" in a voice that sounded as though she wanted to lie down and die.

I knew how she felt. I was dreading going anywhere near our evil stepmother again. I had been hoping that we'd make it through an entire term at Rookwood at least.

I had begged Mrs Knight to telephone Aunt Sara and Aunt Phoebe to see if they could take us. Aunt Sara's telephone was answered by her shop girl, who said she had just left to take her designs to Paris and wouldn't be back for two weeks. Aunt Phoebe's neighbour, who was the only person nearby with a telephone, said that she'd been taken with a bad flu and was on strict bed rest, with orders to avoid spreading it to anyone else.

We were stuck.

I called another emergency meeting of the Whispers on Tuesday evening.

"Are these meetings ever not an emergency?" Penny asked as she slipped into our room, her voice dripping with derision.

I ignored her. "We have three days to find the keys to that safe before we all get shipped off."

"I'm looking forward to going home," Ebony said quietly.

"Me too," said Nadia.

"Well, that makes two of you," I said. The rest of us all looked miserable at the prospect.

Rose stared at the floor. "I don't even have a home to go to."

Violet reached over and took her hand. "You can come with me," she said.

There was another wave of silence before Ariadne stood up with her notebook, her pencil tucked behind her ear.

"We need another plan for how we're going to track down these keys. Or some ideas, at least." She pulled out the pencil and hovered it over the paper. "Anyone?"

You could almost hear everyone's brains working as we sat trying to come up with something.

Ariadne finally had enough of waiting. "All right," she said, "let's try this another way. Where would you hide keys?"

"A wardrobe?" I suggested, staring around our bedroom. "A desk drawer?"

Ariadne was scribbling furiously.

"But then again," I said, recalling what I'd thought when we were searching Matron's apartment, "if they were in a piece of furniture, wouldn't someone have found them by now?"

Ivy's brow wrinkled. "Not necessarily. Remember all that old broken furniture on the third floor, where the Whispers' book was hidden for so many years? Nobody had even thought to look in it."

Ariadne nodded. "And even if someone had found a key, they might not have thought it was important."

"I still think the keys were probably given to different people," said Ebony. "So they could be anywhere by now. And she might have hidden them in more than one place, so it couldn't be easily solved."

"Under the floorboards?" Nadia suggested. "Up a chimney?"

I sighed and put my head in my hands, before looking up again. "So we've narrowed it down to ANYWHERE IN THE WHOLE WORLD."

Ivy patted my shoulder. "Well, if they're not here," she pointed out, "we have no chance anyway. So we have to hope she hid them somewhere in Rookwood."

Ugh. My twin was right. But I didn't want to think about that.

Rose suddenly raised her hand. "Miss Fox," she whispered.

Everyone stared at her. I felt the hairs rise on the back of my neck. "What?"

But Violet started nodding. "Miss Fox had heaps of keys," she explained. "What if the right ones were sitting in her pockets all along?"

"What happened to her keys, though?" Nadia asked. "Did they take them off her at the prison? Or are they here somewhere? We could ask Mrs Knight if she ever got them back."

Ariadne looked up from her writing. "We could check the hexagonal lodge! Miss Fox was hiding out there. She could have left them behind."

"Good idea!" Ivy chimed in.

I was feeling a little less enthusiastic. "I don't think so."
I trawled through my memory. "I think... I think when we
found Miss Finch at the lodge, she said she'd heard the keys
in Miss Fox's pockets as she was leaving. So she probably
still had them with her when she was arrested."

"Oh," everyone said, looking disappointed.

"At this rate all of us will just have to search non-stop."
I pushed out a frustrated breath. "But if that's what it takes,
well..."

"I could try to pick the locks," Ariadne said, chewing the
end of her pencil. "But that would take a lot of time, and
we don't even know if it's possible."

"And there's a combination," I reminded her.

"Oh gosh," she said, frowning and making another note
about that. "I forgot about that. *More* searching required.
This is a puzzle!"

Ebony looked thoughtful. "We put on a play in the
theatre once about an old man who'd hidden his fortune
somewhere, and left clues that only his favourite son could
follow. What if Lady Wootton had thought along the same
lines?"

"You could be right," I replied. "She probably didn't
mean it to be an unsolvable puzzle, just one that would
keep the likes of Mr Bartholomew out. Maybe there're some

clues in that writing about her, the stuff I couldn't decipher."

Ariadne nodded and scribbled another note. "I'll try to get another look at it."

We all smiled at each other hopefully. Perhaps there was something we could do after all. We'd solved difficult puzzles before, hadn't we? And with all of us working together... maybe there was a chance that we'd figure it out before Henry sent us all home. Before Ivy and I were back at the mercy of our stepmother.

I'd been thinking about the mystery of the keys all night. I thought that Rose and Violet might well be on to something with their theory about Miss Fox, and it occurred to me that Miss Finch might have an idea.

On Wednesday morning, while the others were finishing up their breakfast, I decided to run and find her. Luckily, I caught her at the top of the steps that went down to the ballet studio. I heard the sound of her walking stick echoing off the floor before I rounded the corner.

"Morning, Scarlet," she called when she saw me. She looked unusually cheerful.

"Morning, Miss," I replied. "You seem happy."

She smiled. "I feel like a small weight has been lifted. Things are a bit easier today, even with the school closure looming over us. And it's got a bit warmer, which always helps my leg. Did you want me for something? You don't have ballet this morning."

"I know," I said. *As if I don't know when my favourite lesson is!* "This is about the school." I peered around the corridor, making sure there was no one in earshot. "Let's say we found something that might contain useful information, but it's locked—"

"Would it be breaking the school rules to open this thing?" Miss Finch interrupted.

I shook my head. "Nope." I wasn't lying – there were no rules forbidding opening secret safes. I just wouldn't mention that you had to break into Matron's bedroom to find it.

She narrowed her eyes at me, but the happiness remained in her expression. "So what do you need?"

"Well..." I shuffled uncomfortably. "Miss Fox had all those keys. We wondered what happened to them."

"They're here, I think," she said. My face lit up, and she continued. "The police confiscated them from my mother when she was arrested, and gave them back to Mrs Knight."

"Mrs Knight has them?" I gasped. "Do you think she'd give them to me?"

Miss Finch looked sceptical. "The keys to every door in

the school? Probably not, Scarlet. Not unless she accompanies you while you have them."

Drat. It looked like we had some serious persuading to do.

I reported back to Ivy and Ariadne, who I found waiting outside our first lesson.

"I don't think we have a choice," I said. "I think we'll have to explain to Mrs Knight why we need them. Unless we steal them..."

"No stealing," said Ivy. "Unless we really need to."

Ariadne bit her lip. "Oh, I do hope we can talk her into it."

"If we can get a moment to talk to her at all," Ivy said. "Although..." She paused. "Mrs Knight is really cross with Henry. And she did let us talk to Miss Fox. Maybe she will understand."

"I don't think we should admit that we were in Matron's room," Ariadne said. Matron had given everyone quite the lecture about not going anywhere near her belongings, and was pretty explicit about the awful punishments she'd give to anyone who did. "I'd rather not get expelled again!"

I shrugged. "We're all effectively about to be expelled anyway. But I see your point." I picked at the wallpaper in the corridor as I thought about it. "We'll come up with something. We'll say we saw the safe on some old plans, and that's how we know it's there."

Ivy nodded slowly. "That could work. We'll try to corner Mrs Knight at break time."

Break time arrived, and we huddled outside the headmistress's office – Ebony had joined us. This time the door was closed. I knocked and we waited.

When there was no answer, I looked at the others. "She can't *still* be on the telephone, surely?" They shrugged in response. I knocked again.

I could hear the telephone ringing from inside, a sharp trill. Probably more angry parents. But no one seemed to be picking it up.

After we'd been waiting for about five minutes, Miss Bowler came striding by. She frowned at us. "Why are you lurking, girls? Have you been sent to the headmistress?" she demanded.

"No," Ariadne said, shrinking back against the wall. "We haven't broken any rules! Honest!"

I swatted at her to shut her up. "We wanted to go in and ask Mrs Knight a question, that's all, Miss."

"Well, you'll be waiting a while," Miss Bowler said. "She's been given the rest of the week off due to stress. I'm in charge for the next few days." She banged a heavy fist on the door. "And this office is remaining locked!"

Chapter Twenty-three

IVY

We stood, stunned, outside the headmistress's office. Our hopes had been dashed yet again.

Miss Bowler didn't seem to notice. "Oi!" she suddenly yelled at someone down the corridor. She pulled up her whistle and blew it sharply. We all covered our ears. "No running!" And with that she marched off, leaving us to wonder what on earth we could do next.

"We're stuck," Scarlet said, hitting the door with her fist.

Ariadne, who was still pressed against the wall, looked

thoughtful. "Perhaps not. We could come back at night, try to pick the lock and take the keys..."

I waved at Ivy. "Miss Morals here said no stealing."

"Um..." said Ebony. "Stealing might not be necessary."

Scarlet turned to her. "What are you talking about?"

Ebony's usually icy cold skin flushed red. "Remember last term when I said I'd taken the caretaker's keys, and that I was going to give them back?"

Now we all stared at her. "Yes..." I said.

She winced. "I didn't give them back."

Ariadne gasped. Scarlet just rolled her eyes.

"Why not?" I asked.

Ebony held up her hands innocently. "I just forgot about it, what with everything that happened with Muriel. I noticed that the caretaker got a new set of keys not long after, and so I thought he probably wouldn't miss them."

Scarlet put her hand on Ebony's arm. "Never mind all that now. If you have the key to this office, we could be in luck! Do you have them on you?"

Ebony shook her head. "No, they're back in our room."

"We can't risk being caught by Miss Bowler," I said. "She'd probably make us clean the swimming pool again. We really don't have the time for punishments if we're going to get the safe open before we all get sent packing!"

"We'll come back tonight," Scarlet said, keeping her

voice low. "If Ebony can let us into the office, we can search for Miss Fox's keys."

That night, after having filled in the others about our plan, the four of us waited until Rookwood was asleep. The halls lay empty and dark.

Walking the corridors in the dead of night was no longer quite as frightening as it once had been. They were so familiar to me now. We'd uncovered so many of the hidden nooks and crannies. I ran my fingers along the wallpaper and the dusty wood as we crept past, Ariadne going ahead with her candleholder.

There was still peril, though – we could still be caught. If Matron woke up and spotted us, we were in big trouble. Especially Ebony, who already had detention for the whole week with Violet and Nadia.

Even though we were going as quietly as we could, I could hear the shuffle of our footsteps on the floor. Whenever Ebony moved quickly, the ring of keys jangled in her pockets, making Scarlet shudder.

We made it to Mrs Knight's office. After a few quick glances to check that the coast was clear, Ebony pulled the keys out and began trying them one by one. By about the eighth key, there was a click. "It worked!" she whispered, leaning on the handle and opening it up.

We quickly dived inside and shut the door gently behind us. I felt my heart pounding in my chest as I flipped the light switch and the room came into focus.

"Search all the drawers," Scarlet said.

Scarlet and I took the ones in the desk, while Ariadne and Ebony looked in the other drawers and cupboards around the office.

Each one I opened just seemed to be filled with paperwork and pens. But when I knelt down to open the bottom drawer, I saw something underneath the desk.

"Under here!" There was a hook beneath the desk with a large ring on it, similar to the one that Ebony held. But this one was crammed with far more keys. I unhooked it and came back out to get a good look. It was so heavy I had to use two hands.

The keys on it certainly looked like the ones that had belonged to Miss Fox. There were tons of them – big ones, small ones, old and rusty ones.

Scarlet looked down at me. "Oh no," she said. "That's going to take forever, if the right keys are even on there!"

Ariadne came over as I stood up and held out the bunch. "The keys to the safe were fairly small. And they'll be old... but we'll still have to work as quickly as we can."

We hurried out of the office, Ebony locking the door behind us, and headed back upstairs. I carried the heavy keys, trying to keep them still so they wouldn't make such a noise. It was time for the most dangerous part of our plan: getting back into Matron's apartment.

And about now our next distraction needed to happen.

The four of us hid down the hallway and peered at Matron's room. We waved at Penny to show her that we had the keys, and with a nod she made her way to Matron's door. She banged on it repeatedly.

After a while, Matron appeared, her hair in curlers and her eye mask perched on her forehead. She yawned. "What is it, Miss Winchester?"

"It's Nadia," Penny said. "She's been sick."

Matron frowned. "Oh goodness. Let me get my clean-up bag."

As Penny led Matron away down the corridor towards the lavatories, we all ran out as quietly as we could. Thankfully, Scarlet just managed to stick her hand in the door and keep it open before it locked – saving us valuable time trying to find the right key.

"Ouch," she whispered, shaking her hand as we piled inside.

We had to work quickly. We ran through to Matron's bedroom, where her bedclothes were unmade after she'd just been rudely awoken. Rushing to the painting of Lady Wootton, we lifted it off the wall together and set it down.

I pulled open the small white door and began trying the

keys, starting with the smallest ones that looked as though they might fit. Ariadne held her candle over me so I could see what I was doing. By the flickering light, I pushed each one in. Some of them wouldn't fit at all, while others were tantalisingly close to fitting, but then wouldn't turn.

"Hurry, hurry," said Ariadne, hopping from one foot to the other.

Scarlet grabbed her arm. "Stop it, Ariadne! You're making the light jump!"

"Sorry!" Ariadne stopped, though her arm was still quivering and the candlelight shook over the keys. "But we could get caught at any moment."

"I'll keep an eye out," said Ebony, running back to the main door.

I tried key after key, but nothing was working, and they were all beginning to blur into one. I was seriously starting to worry that we had completely the wrong idea.

And then suddenly...

Click.

"That's it!" Scarlet exclaimed. "That's the one!"

I peered closely at the key. It was brass, fairly small, and definitely old. I twisted and pulled it back out, and then held it up to the light. There, in very small letters on the top, I could just make out a tiny stamp of three initials. "EMW", once again.

"Look!" I pointed at the stamp. "It's labelled!" Keeping

hold of the first key, I began frantically flicking through them to see if there was another.

"Here!" Scarlet grabbed one and lifted it up. It was a perfect match. I let her take the ring from me, and she tried this one in the second lock.

Click.

"Yes!" Ariadne exclaimed, still wobbling. "Do we have the last one?"

We all pored over the keys. This time we dropped to the ground, putting the candleholder down between us, and each began going through them.

"I'm not seeing it," Scarlet said, an air of worry in her voice.

"Me neither," I replied. A dreadful feeling began to creep in. "I don't think it's here..."

We were stuck without the third key, and with no combination either.

Just then, Ebony came skidding into the room. "Matron's coming back!" she hissed.

With panicked glances at each other, Scarlet and I jumped up. Scarlet handed Ebony the keys and then we slammed the door on the safe, and began lifting the picture back into position.

But just as we did so, we heard the apartment door open.

Before we could think what to do, Matron appeared in her bedroom doorway.

Chapter Twenty-four

SCARLET

"What in heaven's name are you doing?" Matron cried when she saw the four of us standing under her painting.

"April Fool?" I tried.

She stared at me like I was mad. "It's not even April!"

"Miss," Ariadne said, pushing me aside, "we got scared. Because... because Nadia was ill. And well, the four of us aren't feeling so good either."

Immediately we all tried to look a bit green. Ivy clutched

her stomach with one hand. I tried to brush my dusty hands on the back of my nightgown.

Ebony nodded. "What if it's a plague, Miss?" She had the keys hidden behind her.

"Why on earth would that mean you had to come into my bedroom?" Matron demanded.

Ariadne's eyes darted frantically as she tried to think of something. "Well, um, we were frightened and we wanted to come and tell you, but when we got here the door was open and we thought perhaps *you'd* come down with the plague as well."

Ivy's head bobbed up and down in agreement. "We were so worried, we just thought we should come in and see if you were all right."

I couldn't tell if Matron believed us, but her frown was slowly softening. "*Really*, girls?"

Desperate, Ariadne threw herself forward and hugged Matron. "We're so glad you're all right!" she said, her voice muffled in Matron's shoulder. Matron stood there agape, her arms still spread out wide. After a few moments she patted Ariadne on the back.

"There, there," she said. "Calm down, Flitworth. There isn't a plague of any sort. Nadia probably just ate too many sweets. What am I always telling you girls about all that sugar?"

"Ohhh," Ariadne stood back, fake relief on her face. "Well, we did eat a lot of sweets," she said. Although, for once, this wasn't true.

Matron yawned, but then her brow furrowed again. "This is a bit ridiculous, girls. In future, if you're feeling unwell and you can't find me, you go straight to Nurse Gladys; understood?"

"Yes, Miss," we all said with enthusiasm. What Matron didn't know was that our enthusiasm was just based on the prospect of getting out of there as soon as possible without getting expelled.

For a moment, she said nothing and just stared at us as if she couldn't quite believe how stupid we were. *Please believe it*, I thought.

"Right, then," she said. "All of you, back to bed. I'm sure you'll feel fine in the morning."

"Yes, Miss," we said again, and began hurrying out – Ebony neatly switching hands so that the heavy bunch of keys was now in front of her and out of Matron's sight.

She turned to us. "And if I catch any of you in here again... there'll be big trouble!"

The four of us collapsed in a heap back in room thirteen.

"My head is spinning," I said, sitting on the floor and leaning against my bed.

Ariadne sneezed. "I think some of it is the dust," she said.

Ebony dropped the keys on to the carpet with a *thud*. "We have two keys that work, and a million that don't."

I sighed and pulled my blanket over my head. "Tell me something I don't know."

"Come on," said Ivy, tugging the blanket away. "We got somewhere. We've *almost* opened the safe."

"*Almost* is good for nothing if we never find the third key and the combination," I said. "We have two days before Henry kicks us all out of school. If he finds the will before us, we've got no other chance. We're—"

"In a bit of a pickle," Ariadne finished, in a much milder fashion than I would have.

"Just a bit," Ivy said.

But Ebony was staring down at the ring where it had fallen. "I can take the keys!" she suddenly exclaimed.

We all looked at her.

"I can take them home to the theatre," she said. "Mrs Knight isn't here, so she won't notice they're gone. So even if Henry finds the safe, he won't be able to open it. Assuming there aren't any copies of the keys, that is."

I thought about it for a moment. Ebony was new to our group, and she'd been untrustworthy before. But hadn't she proved herself enough? "Okay," I said, eventually. "Good idea." The others nodded.

Ariadne's eyelids were fluttering open and shut. "I need to sleep," she said.

"Right," I said through a yawn, "everyone get out of here and into bed. Well, not Ivy, you live here. But you two." I waved at Ariadne and Ebony. "We'll fill in the others tomorrow. Maybe they'll have some more ideas..."

As Ivy and I curled up in our beds, the wind howling through the trees outside as the rain began to pick up, I tried to think where the final key might be. But after what seemed like only moments, I was fast asleep.

The next morning at breakfast, Ariadne was carrying a paper folder under her arm as we queued for our daily Rookwood porridge.

I peered at it, still a little bleary-eyed. "What is that?"

"It's the old writings about the school. I went to the library again and persuaded Miss Jones to let me take these away," she said, blowing a lock of hair from her forehead. "It wasn't easy, but thankfully I have a perfect track record of returning everything I borrow in tip-top condition." She grinned.

Ivy yawned down at her tray. "I don't know how you're so awake, Ariadne."

I nodded in agreement. "I can't believe you got up early enough to go to the library before you even had breakfast."

"It's the pursuit of knowledge," Ariadne said brightly. "It's invigorating!"

"If you say so," I said as the cook spooned a helping of lumpy porridge into my bowl. I'd never felt less invigorated in my life.

As we ate, we spread the word to the others about what we'd found. Unfortunately, the whispered words got a bit garbled along the way.

"You found some great cheese?" Penny asked, her nose wrinkling.

"The *safe keys*," Ebony hissed.

"*Ohh!*"

I rolled my eyes and started writing down a note on a piece of scrap paper to pass along instead. At least everyone would get the right message, then. We needed every brain we had thinking about this problem if we were to have any chance.

IMPORTANT
We found two of the right safe keys!
Still need last one and the combination.
got caught but just about got away
with it...
Look everywhere for keys with EMW on!
Meet this evening to discuss ideas.

Pass this on.
MUST NOT GET CAUGHT AGAIN!

I folded it up and passed it to Penny, then watched the wide-eyed reactions of the others as they read it.

I spent every lesson that day thinking about keys. Had Lady Wootton hidden them, or kept them on her person? Either way, we knew Miss Fox had acquired them, even if she didn't know what they were for, just as she'd acquired the keys to almost every lock in the school. So why hadn't she found the third one? Was it hidden somewhere even *she* wouldn't have thought to look?

I had hidden a key myself, once, when I was leaving a trail for Ivy in the hope that she'd find out what Miss Fox had done to me. It was for a locker and I'd hidden it inside the skull of Wilhelmina, the skeleton that lived in the biology cupboard. Supposedly, Wilhelmina was a past student of Rookwood. I had never been sure if the teachers were lying about that, but I didn't really want to find out.

But the point was, keys like the ones used in the safe and the lockers were small and you could hide them almost anywhere. We looked in the classroom desks, and even peered in the teachers' desks after each lesson. We opened any cupboards that we could find. We opened *anything* that could possibly have contained a key. I was sure I was going to be drowning in keys in my dreams.

By the time we met up in room thirteen at the end of the day, we'd found:

- Three locker keys
- Two large door keys
- One tiny key that looked like it was for a lockable journal
- Two keys for a suitcase

Unfortunately, these were all less than useless. Well, except for one of the suitcase keys, which turned out to be one of Ariadne's that she'd lost. But other than that, they were all the wrong size, and not one of them was stamped with EMW.

"Right," I said, looking down at the small pile on our carpet. "So this was a waste of time. Anyone got any better ideas?"

"We can keep searching," said Violet, "but we have nothing to go on again. We need a lead if we're going to get anywhere."

I gave an exasperated sigh. At least we would be able to get the first two keys away from Henry – that was something. But I wouldn't put it past him to get someone to come and drill the safe out of the wall if he actually found it. We didn't have long left and he would get every chance to search for it while the school was empty.

"*Does* anyone have any ideas?" Ivy asked desperately.

There was a slow shaking of heads.

I curled my hands into fists. "Then we keep looking," I said. But would it do any good?

Friday dawned. It was our last day, and our last chance before Henry had us all thrown out for the next week.

We looked everywhere else we could think of – any stone that had been unturned was turned. But soon something became clear: we were not going to find the key before we were all sent away.

We were out of time.

Chapter Twenty-five

IVY

That Saturday morning at Rookwood School was one of the wildest I'd ever seen. Girls were racing back and forth across the hallway, into each other's rooms. Some of them were crying, others were laughing and gossiping about what they'd be doing with their week off.

Scarlet and I were just sitting in a sort of numb silence. Our bags were packed and ready. All we could do was sit and wait for Father to turn up and bring us home.

When the time neared, we pushed out into the crowds

and dragged our things downstairs, meeting Ariadne and Ebony on the way.

"I can't believe it," Ariadne said quietly as we helped her pull her luggage towards the foyer. "This might really be the end. If Henry gets to the safe and it has the real will inside... we've truly lost the school forever."

Scarlet shushed her, looking around in case he was lurking anywhere nearby. But he'd surely have needed superhuman hearing to pick out anything over the din that was flooding the halls.

There was a huge queue snaking from the front door as people filtered out. We shuffled forward slowly until we were actually inside the entrance hall. Miss Bowler was presiding over the whole thing, looking very much like she'd rather be anywhere else.

"QUIETLY!" she bellowed, ironically. "And quickly! No loitering! Wait outside, find your parents and be off!" She waved in the direction of the front door as if she were shooing rats.

Ariadne sighed. "I hope Mrs Knight will be back next term."

"If there *is* a next term," Scarlet said darkly.

At that moment, though, I was a little less concerned about the school and a little more concerned about what was going to happen to us. In a strange way I was looking forward to seeing Father again, but at the same time I feared he would be just as odd and distant as he had been before. And our stepmother, well... there was no telling what she would do. But you could always guarantee that, whatever it was, it would be awful.

When we were finally outside the front doors, we were met with a blustery day and the engine exhaust from the endless motor cars that were filling up the drive. Girls spilt out on to the grass in front of the school, desperately clinging to their hats and bags as the wind tried its best to steal them.

With some effort we managed to track down the rest of the Whispers. Scarlet waved us round and we huddled together.

"Maybe this is the end," she said.

"Cheerful," Penny interjected.

"Let me finish!" Scarlet barked. "*Maybe* this is the end, but we just have to hope that Henry won't figure out what he needs to look for – and find the safe. And even if he does, Ebony has two of the keys..." Ebony nodded. "So perhaps that'll at least slow him down."

There was a pause, and then Ariadne wailed, "*I don't want to leave!*"

I patted her on the back.

Scarlet did the same. "We'll be back in a week," she

reassured her. "I don't care if Henry wants to flatten the school to the ground. I'll chain myself to the front door!"

"I thought you hated Rookwood," Violet said to my twin. "You were always complaining."

"Yes," said Scarlet. "But I hate Henry even more. He can have this school over my dead body, the smarmy weasel."

As if on cue, a tall figure pushed his way out of the doors and stood on the steps, clearing his throat loudly. *Henry*.

"Good morning, girls," he said without a trace of irony. "I hope you'll enjoy your well-deserved break."

"BOO!" Scarlet heckled, but I shushed her. I wanted to hear what he had to say. We broke up our group so we could listen to him.

"I just want to reassure you – and your parents," he added, gesturing at the adults who were standing beside their cars and peering at him curiously, their dresses and ties being pulled about by the wind. "That this is just a routine investigation into the safety of the school. Nothing to worry about!"

Henry seemed as calm and nonchalant as ever, despite the hundreds of eyes that were glaring at him. I don't think anyone trusted him now. We all knew our school was under threat, no matter what he said.

"The building needs repairs," he continued. "This is all for your safety and comfort, I promise you that. Now, I'm not saying that the building will definitely need to be torn down..."

"*Really?*" Scarlet said beside me, her arms folded. "You're *not* saying that?"

Henry was thankfully too far away to hear this. "But if it does, well..." He shrugged and grinned. "What can you do? I promise I will do my absolute best to save this school. For all of you." He raised his hands as if he were some sort of divine prophet sent to rescue us all.

More boos rang out from the crowd, and a few hisses. One girl tried to throw a ball of paper at him.

The parents, though, didn't seem so bothered. Several of them shushed their protesting daughters.

"That sounds all right," I heard a bearded man say. "This old building looks in need of it."

"Better safe than sorry," a woman said, clinging to her flowery hat that was threatening to escape.

Henry clapped his hands together. "Thank you so much, everyone! I'll be seeing you all again soon." Even from a distance, I could see the sparkle in his dark eyes. He ran a hand through his hair and then disappeared back inside the school.

"Ariadne, darling!" I heard someone call. "Yoo-hoo!"

As the line of motor cars began to move along, we saw Ariadne's father leaning from the window of one of them.

He climbed out and came over to us. "Good morning, Sally and Irene," he said to us, tipping his hat. He never could get our names right. "Jolly funny business, this, isn't it?"

Ariadne suddenly hugged him, clinging on to his tweed suit.

"Oh," he said. He looked rather baffled as he gently patted her on the back. "Is something the matter, dear?"

Ariadne pulled back and sniffed. "No," she said. "I just don't want to leave."

He gave her another puzzled expression and wiped his glasses. "It's only a week, dearest. You heard the gentleman. Safety is of the utmost importance. I keep telling you this school isn't safe! I don't know how you persuaded us to send you back here. Honestly, is this place even up to regulations? And my goodness, those headteachers..."

He kept talking as he led her away to the car. Ariadne looked back at us helplessly, and we waved at her, mouthing goodbyes. The rest of the Whispers began to filter away too, looking for their parents.

My heart sank as I saw our father's car approaching. This was where it ended. We were going home to our stepmother.

Father was still acting strangely on the way home. He flitted between asking us questions about school (something he rarely did) and staring silently as he drove. A few times, he had to swerve to avoid something: a pothole, a rabbit, a branch in the road. Once he even swerved when there was nothing there to see. We nearly crashed into the hedge.

When we were about halfway home, he suddenly pulled over at the side of the road. His palms were sweating as he gripped the wheel tightly.

"What's wrong?" Scarlet asked, but he just shook his head and blinked. When he finally turned to us, he was white, like he'd seen a ghost.

"Emmeline?" he whispered.

Scarlet frowned, and I paled. He was talking about our mother, using her false name – the one she'd used when he knew her.

"She's dead, Father," Scarlet said, never one to be tactful.

Father turned back to the road. "Who's dead?" he asked, pulling away again as if nothing had happened.

Despite all this, we managed to get back home without further incident. Father got out of the driver's seat and headed straight for the house as if we weren't even there.

Scarlet leant over. "What's wrong with him?" she asked under her breath.

"I don't know, but I think he's getting worse," I replied. "We need to keep an eye on him."

She nodded, and we both scrambled out of the car with our bags.

There was the house again: the pretty cottage, covered in thorns. At least the frost had gone from the air.

As we trod up the path, I saw that the front door was swinging open. I pushed through. It was cold, quiet and a little dark inside.

"Did Father go to his office?" Scarlet asked, dropping her bag on to the hallway floor.

I put mine down beside it. "Maybe," I said.

We headed in that direction, to find that this door was also wide open, with no one inside.

Now I was frowning. "This is odd." When Father was at home, he was almost always in his office.

We checked the whole downstairs and even the outhouse, but there was no sign of Father. That meant venturing upstairs. We picked up our bags and took them up to our bedroom, the one that looked as though it hadn't been touched in ten years.

The room that Father shared with Edith was just along the hall, and again the door wasn't shut – though this time there was only a crack where it hadn't quite stuck in the frame. With a nervous glance at my twin, I pushed it open.

And there was Father, collapsed on the bed, still wearing his suit and shoes.

Chapter Twenty-six

SCARLET

"This is not like him," Ivy said.

Once we'd determined that our father was not in fact dead, but merely sleeping, we were still concerned. I gingerly felt his forehead to find it cold and clammy. He didn't seem well.

I shook my head. I really didn't know what to do. "Let's just leave him to sleep. He's been working a lot. Maybe it's exhaustion."

Ivy didn't look at all convinced, but she agreed and we tiptoed out of the room.

We went back downstairs, hoping to find some food, but instead we were met with a less than appetising sight: our stepmother.

She was herding our stepbrothers in through the front door. They were looking taller and scruffier than ever.

"Hello," Ivy tried.

I instantly wished she hadn't said anything. Edith regarded us on the stairs and looked as if we'd just threatened to stab her. The boys, on the other hand, all pulled *eurgh* faces and ran away. Did they ever stand still?

"Well," said Edith, hands on her hips. "You're here again. That's strange, because I distinctly remember telling you that you were not welcome here."

"We didn't have a choice," I told her, gripping the banister tightly.

"Our school is closed for the week," Ivy explained. "Father brought us back."

"Nice of him to tell me," she muttered under her breath. Then she looked up at us again. "You two had better make yourselves useful." She shot out her arm towards the kitchen. "Clean up. Dust. Sweep the fireplaces."

I felt myself deflating. More of this! "And what will the boys be doing?" I asked sarcastically. "Arranging flowers?"

Our stepmother ignored me. "Listen, you little brats," she hissed, pointing at me and shaking with anger. "I don't want you here, and you don't want to be here. But if you have to be under my roof, you do as I say."

I folded my arms. "You wouldn't talk to us like that if Father were here."

Her frown deepened even further. "And where is he?"

"He's upstairs," Ivy said, with a concerned glance at me. "He just fell asleep. Is he all right?"

"Oh," Edith said. Her expression became unreadable. Then she waved the question away. "He's fine, I'm sure. Probably exhausted from dealing with you two."

I didn't know what to say. *Dealing* with us? We hadn't done anything!

"What are you waiting for?" she barked. "Kitchen, now!"

We trudged slowly towards the kitchen like we were going to a funeral. I resisted the urge to punch our stepmother as we went past.

"At least if we're alone doing all the cleaning, we don't have to look at her," I whispered to Ivy.

We got started. We swept the floors, cleaned the dishes, dusted the cobwebs. Everything was filthy. I thought our stepmother might have deliberately left it all in that state just to make us sort it out, but according to her she hadn't even known we were coming. She was probably lying.

It was when I was cleaning the spice rack that I found it.

The spice rack had belonged to our mother. It hung on the wall near the oven, and was filled with all manner of herbs and spices in jars that mostly looked like they hadn't been touched since she'd died. But there were a few on the bottom, like the salt and pepper, that were less dusty and seemed still to be in use. I ran a cloth over them, not really paying attention to the monotonous task, when a jam jar labelled HERBS went crashing off the shelf and smashed into pieces on the floor.

"Drat! Did she hear that?" I said. Ivy and I froze, waiting for thundering footsteps to come down the hall, but there was nothing.

"I'll clean it up," Ivy said, fetching the dustpan and brush for the glass. But I'd noticed something.

The jar hadn't been empty. Nor had it been filled with herbs. In fact, it contained a small black bottle, which somehow was still intact. It had a plain label.

Crouching down, I carefully picked it up from the shards surrounding it. "What...?" I muttered. I unscrewed the cap and was met with a faint smell that I couldn't quite place.

I peered inside. It was filled with white powder. It looked like crushed tablets of some sort. "Ivy..."

She got down to my level and looked at the bottle in my hands. "What is it?"

I bit my lip. "I don't know. But I don't think it's herbs."

Ivy paled and began to sweep up the glass, which crunched under the brush.

I was still staring at the bottle. As I looked more closely, I saw that the blank white label was coming away slightly in one corner. Was it covering something? I stood up and picked at it until, after some effort, it peeled off in one go. I dropped it to the floor.

There was another label underneath it, one that someone had clearly tried unsuccessfully to remove. But you could just make out the remains in red ink: a skull and crossbones, and the word POISON.

I couldn't breathe. My free hand clamped over my mouth. *Poison. Our stepmother had poison.*

What was she going to do with it? What *had* she done?

Carefully, as if I were disposing of a bomb, I screwed the cap back on and set the thing down on the table.

I turned round to see Ivy wrapping the glass shards in newspaper and throwing them in the dustbin. She took one look at me, and I thought she was going to drop everything. "Scarlet? What's wrong?"

She walked back over. With a shaking hand, I pointed to the black bottle on the table. "It's poison," I said.

"*What?* Are you sure?" She leant closer, and I watched her expression as she read the label. As she straightened up, it was like looking at a ghost of myself in the mirror. I imagined both of us were as pale as each other. "Maybe it's for rats..." she tried.

I shook my head. "It was in a herb jar, Ivy! And its label was covered!"

Ivy's eyes were wide and scared. "She wouldn't..."

Now I could feel my fear turning to anger. "She would. She pretended I was dead just because Miss Fox gave her money! She planned my fake funeral! And now she wants to make it a reality!"

Ivy's hands flew up to her face. "You think she means *to kill us*?"

"I wouldn't be surprised," I growled, clenching my fists.

But something else was coming into my mind.

Father.

For months, he'd been acting strangely. He hadn't been himself at all. I thought he was just distracted by what he'd learnt about our mother. But now... now everything was worse. He'd nearly crashed the car on the way home. Now he was collapsed upstairs, white-faced and cold.

The same idea seemed to occur to Ivy at the same time. "You don't think..."

"Father—" I began.

"She's already doing it," Ivy finished. "She's putting this in his food!"

Ivy was right, I was sure of it. Our stepmother wasn't just nasty, she was truly evil.

For a moment I had the urge to pick up the tiny black bottle and hurl it at the wall, smashing it to pieces. But I didn't – I didn't want to breathe in any of that white powder and, besides, it was evidence.

Ivy started pacing frantically. "We need to stop this, right now! But how can we?"

I couldn't take my eyes from the bottle. An idea was beginning to form in my mind.

"We put it back," I said.

Ivy stopped and looked up at me in surprise. "What?"

"We put it back," I repeated. "We'll replace the jam jar and make it look like the one that got smashed. Then she won't know any different."

"Why?" Ivy asked, her hands spread wide, her eyes looking at me like I'd just suggested we both volunteer to be murdered.

"Because –" I said, unclenching my fists, letting the anger turn into something new – "we're going to catch her red-handed."

Chapter Twenty-seven

IVY

We did just as Scarlet had planned. I found a nearly empty jam jar in a cupboard, washed it out and made a new label.

"Shouldn't we run for the doctor?" I asked as I did this. I was now seriously worried about Father. He could be useless and uncaring at times, but he was still our father. I didn't want him to die.

"If we do that," Scarlet warned, "she'll be on to us straight away. She'll probably throw out the evidence and lie to the doctor. If we can expose what she's up to in front of Father, then we'll be free to help him."

I thought she was probably right, but there was still so much that could go wrong. How ill was Father, really? We had no idea what this poison was, or how long Edith had been giving it to him.

"We'll just have to pray she tries it tonight," I said. But to myself, I added – *If she doesn't, then maybe I'll just call for the doctor anyway*. We couldn't let this go on any longer. Maybe it would backfire and Father would never forgive us, but at least he would be seen by someone.

We carefully re-covered the label on the little black bottle, and put it inside the new jar. Then we replaced it on the spice rack. It barely looked any different from how it had before.

"She isn't getting away with this," Scarlet said. "No matter what she tries. We'll stop her."

I wished I had my sister's confidence, but since we'd as good as lost against Henry Bartholomew, and we'd never once managed to reveal our stepmother's true colours in the past... I didn't have much hope.

People rarely listened to us until it was too late.

I was barely keeping it together as we came back downstairs that evening. We'd heard our stepmother banging about in the kitchen – which meant she was cooking. We had to get down there to watch her.

I stepped inside, and as soon as she saw me, she snapped, "Ivy! You need to chop these vegetables. Now."

I nodded and got to work. If she thought I was helping, she wouldn't kick me out.

Scarlet, on the other hand, had gone to fetch Father. He'd just woken up in his bedroom, and seemed to be all right – for now. Our plan was to get him to sit in the kitchen, so he could witness what was happening.

"Where are the boys?" I asked Edith.

She frowned at me, appearing shocked that I'd spoken to her at all. "They've gone for tea with their friends," she said.

"Ah," I said, carefully chopping a carrot. That was good. I didn't really want them here to see this.

Not long afterwards, Father appeared, yawning, in the doorway, with Scarlet behind him. He sat at the table and peered at his newspaper as if it were first thing in the morning.

I shared a fearful glance with Scarlet. I felt as though we were teetering on the brink. So much could go wrong. What if our stepmother didn't use the poison in front of us? We needed to keep a close watch.

She was bustling around, putting salt on a piece of meat,

stirring a sauce angrily (I hadn't known that you could stir a sauce angrily, but our stepmother definitely managed it). And then she went over to the spice rack...

"Ouch!"

I'd been so busy watching her that I hadn't been looking down at my hands, and I'd cut my finger with the knife. It stung, a small drop of blood sliding down my skin.

Edith looked at me in horror. "You clumsy—" she began, before realising that she was about to insult me in front of Father. "Get yourself cleaned up."

Drat. I'd stopped her from picking up the poison! I went over to the sink and washed my finger, putting pressure on the cut so that it would stop bleeding. It was thankfully only small. But had our plan been thwarted?

Edith turned round to my twin. "You. Scarlet. Finish the chopping."

Scarlet came over and carried on. We shared a glance, wondering what would happen next. Every time I looked back at Father, he seemed in a little less of a daze.

When the food was nearly ready, our stepmother made us get the plates out. I was really beginning to worry. We needed her to pick up the poison, or our whole plan was out of the window. We bustled around the kitchen, trying our best to watch our stepmother like a hawk.

And then it happened.

Standing over one of the plates, the one with the largest portion of meat that was reserved for Father, our stepmother was once again reaching for the jar. I could barely breathe as she picked it up, her claw-like fingers closing round the outside. Would she notice that it was different?

But she said nothing. With a quick glance over her shoulder, she unscrewed the lid.

Scarlet was closest. She ran forward and grabbed our stepmother's arm, holding it outstretched. "Stop!" she yelled.

"WHAT ARE YOU DOING?" our stepmother roared. She tried to wriggle free, but Scarlet had a tough grip.

Father finally looked up from his newspaper, frowning. "Scarlet? What on earth..."

"She's trying to poison you!" Scarlet all but screamed.

"I've never heard such nonsense in all my life!" Edith protested. Her cheeks were turning red. "Unhand me this instant, you horrible child!"

Father's frown deepened. "Let go of her, Scarlet," he said. Even this hadn't brought back his fire. He still sounded flat and empty, not able to summon the energy to shout.

I had to do something. I dashed over to them and pulled the jar from our stepmother's fingers, so that Father could clearly see what I was doing. Edith was shaking with rage. I half thought she might spit in my eye.

Hurrying to the table, with Father watching me intently, I put the jar down and pulled out the black bottle. The label we'd replaced peeled off easily, revealing the POISON warning.

In that moment, everything seemed to slow down. There was something in Father's eyes that I hadn't seen for years and years. It was as if he was suddenly truly awake.

He turned to our stepmother at a glacial pace. "What is this?" he said, barely raising his voice.

"It's a trick!" she screeched. "They did this!" She swung her free arm back and forth between Scarlet and me.

"We think this is why you've been feeling unwell," I said, trying to ignore her.

"They're only herbs!" Edith protested.

"I thought..." said Father, staring down at the table. "I thought my food had been tasting a little off. I *thought* I was imagining it." He put his hand to his forehead. It was like the realisation was truly hitting him. "Edith... Why?"

She was getting frantic now, and finally wrenched her arm away from Scarlet. There was a red mark where my twin had gripped her. "Honestly, Mortimer, these little brats have hated me since the day I first arrived! Can't you see that?"

Father's gaze didn't waver, but I could see the hurt in his eyes. "I didn't ask you that, Edith, I asked you *why*. After all we've been through together, all I've done for you!"

"And I've told you it's nonsense," said Edith.

"You have no other reason to have poison," he replied. "And certainly not to be hiding it among the herbs."

"She wants you dead!" Scarlet said. "Just like she wants us out of the way!"

Our stepmother turned to Scarlet, her fury radiating from her. "I don't regret letting that woman lock you away for one second," she hissed. "It was worth every penny. I wish you had been gone forever!"

She froze, then. I felt something wrench at my heart and I realised what had just happened.

She'd just admitted what she'd done.

She *had* accepted Miss Fox's bribe. She *knew* Scarlet was locked in the asylum. She knew my twin wasn't really dead, but she'd made us believe it anyway.

And now Father knew the truth.

He stood up. "Get out," he said.

She pressed herself against the kitchen counter, her eyes wide. "What did you say?"

Father didn't back down. "You heard me. I said *get out*."

"Mortimer, this is my – our home..."

"You forfeited that when YOU LET ME THINK MY DAUGHTER WAS DEAD AND THEN TRIED TO MURDER ME!" Father roared, so loudly that I flinched.

Edith looked afraid, but her eyes slowly narrowed, her old

stubbornness coming back. "Oh, you think you're so wonderful? I work here every day, cleaning and cooking and raising the boys! And what thanks do I get in return? I know what you've been keeping from me, Mortimer." She tapped her nose. "I found out how much you've been earning. Why haven't I seen a penny? Why do I have to scrimp and save?"

"Or accept bribes from evil teachers?" Scarlet added sarcastically, but they ignored her.

"I gave you enough," Father said. "I cared for you! I gave you a roof over your head!"

"I want a *way of life*!" she seethed, jabbing her finger at him. "I want what you did for your precious Emmeline, or whatever her name was! You hear two words about her and suddenly you're *obsessed* again!"

Father clenched his fists. He hated it when people brought up our mother. "Stop changing the subject."

"This *is* the subject!" Edith shot back. "Why do you think I did this?"

There was near-silence again, heavy with tension. All that could be heard was the crackle from the dying embers of the fire. So *that* was why she wanted to get rid of Father? She was angry about Mother, and not being given enough money – so she was going to *kill* him to get what she thought she deserved? My mind could scarcely contain it. I felt my legs shaking beneath me.

Eventually, Father walked over to her. I watched her cower. He wouldn't hurt her, I knew, but I'd never seen him so furious in my life.

"You need to leave," he said, his quavering voice barely containing his rage. "You have two hours. Fetch your boys, gather your things and GET. OUT." He flung his arm towards the door.

"But—"

"If I ever see you again I will call the police immediately," he said. "Now LEAVE."

We watched as our stepmother, finally speechless, her futile protests dying on her lips, gave us one last hateful look.

And then the bittersweet moment we'd dreamt of for years finally happened.

She left.

Chapter Twenty-eight

SCARLET

I should have felt happy.

This was what I'd always wanted, wasn't it? To expose the truth about our stepmother? For Father to see who she really was? I thought it would be like throwing a bucket of water on the Wicked Witch – she'd melt away and we'd all celebrate.

Instead, she'd left us in a mess, Father sick and devastated, the two of us feeling just as queasy.

Would she really leave? Would we truly be free of her forever?

Father was silent, slumped in his chair. Ivy and I were sitting beside him, wondering what on earth we should do next. I could hear Edith stomping around before she flew out of the door, slamming it behind her. She must have been going to get the boys.

"Father?" Ivy said carefully after a while. "I think you need a doctor."

He shook his head slowly. "I just... I need..."

Ivy looked up at me. *Go*, I mouthed. There was nothing stopping us now. Father still didn't look well, and I wasn't going to leave again without knowing that he would be all right.

Ivy got up and went to get her coat. Our family doctor was Dr Bevan, and he lived in the village. It wouldn't take long for him to get here.

Just as I thought that, Father slumped forward on to the table.

"Ivy!" I cried out. "Quickly!"

She peered back in and saw what I was looking at. Within seconds, she was running for the door.

It didn't take long for Dr Bevan to arrive with his medical bag and his bushy eyebrows pulled together in a worried frown. He managed to wake Father again, and got him upstairs to bed. We had handed him the poison bottle and waited anxiously for the verdict. Ivy sat down while I paced the room. The food that had been prepared for dinner sat cold and uneaten.

The doctor eventually came back downstairs to the kitchen. "He should be fine," he said, and we both breathed a sigh of relief. "I don't think he's ingested enough of the stuff to do any permanent damage. He will have to rest for several days, and I've given him some medicine to clear out his system."

"Thank you," I breathed. I'd been much more afraid than I'd realised.

Dr Bevan nodded stiffly. He was never one to make much small talk. "You did well to call me when you did. This could have got much worse – your father has assured me that he will have the police look into this as soon as he's up to it."

I glanced at Ivy, but she didn't meet my eye. I wasn't sure if she'd told him that our stepmother was the one to blame. Maybe she hadn't. I think she thought Father should be the one to report her.

For the first time I began to wonder what had really happened to her previous husband. Had she poisoned him too?

"Keep an eye on him," Dr Bevan said finally, before heading for the door.

"Thank you so much," Ivy said again, and he gave her a small smile as he left.

I looked down at the food in front of us. "I can't bring myself to eat it now," I said.

"I know what you mean," said Ivy. "I don't feel hungry after this."

I sighed. "Let's just clean up." At least nobody was ordering us to do it now.

The following few days were very strange. Our stepmother brought her boys back that evening, and we could hear them banging about as they gathered their belongings.

"But where are we going?" I heard Harry ask as they passed our bedroom.

"To Grandma's," Edith barked. "Hurry up."

We kept out of their way. I resisted the urge to go and shout at her. Or something worse.

After that, the house was filled with quiet. We kept checking on Father, and bringing him soup and water. He was still in a bit of a daze, but each day he was looking better. His skin began to get its colour back, and he seemed more and more present.

It was a little strange to have to fend for ourselves, but since our stepmother had usually forced us to do everything anyway, it didn't make much of a difference.

*

The day came when Father was up and about. Over breakfast that morning, he finally talked to us properly.

"Girls..." he said as he sat down.

We both looked up from our toast and eggs. I was immediately worried about where this was going.

"Can you ever forgive me?" he asked.

I nearly spat out my food, but I remembered to chew and swallow.

"Sorry?" Ivy asked, sounding as shocked as I was.

He shook his head. "I am so sorry. I've let you both down."

We were both gaping at him. Father had barely said two words to us in years that weren't about school or something else boring and unimportant. This was the last thing I expected.

He seemed to realise we weren't going to speak, so he carried on explaining. "When I lost your mother... I felt as though I'd lost everything. And I had to bear that weight while I raised twin girls by myself." He shook his head slowly. "For a long time I was angry about it, but then for years, I've... I've been... numb. It was the only way I could keep going."

I thought I was beginning to see what he was getting at. "And this was a wake-up call?" I asked.

He paused a moment. "Yes. Edith came along at just the

right time – or the wrong time, perhaps. She helped me and she kept the house and I thought that was enough. Until now."

Ivy had tears in her eyes. "But everything that she did to us..."

"I know," Father said. "That's why I'm sorry. I didn't see it. It was right in front of my eyes and I didn't see it." He hit the table with his fist, making us jump. "I... I started to feel differently once I learnt the truth about your mother from your Aunt Sara. It reminded me of how much I cared for Emmeline – for Ida, or whatever I should call her. It reminded me of how much I cared for both of you."

Now I was tearing up as well. "Father, I—"

"It's all right, Scarlet," he said, looking at me, and for the first time since I was a young child I felt he was really seeing us. "I don't think I can ever make this right. I would have lost you forever if Edith and that headmistress had pulled off their plan. And if I'd continued to ignore what Edith was up, to I would be dead." He shrugged after saying that as if he'd accepted it.

"We tried to tell you," Ivy said quietly.

His frown deepened. "I've been a fool. A total and utter fool. I should have listened. I should have been there." Now he leant forward and reached for both of our hands across the table. It felt so strange, but there was a rush of this unfamiliar sensation as if a missing piece of me had been put back, just like it had when I was reunited with Ivy. "We need to be a family again," Father continued. "But I'll understand if you can't forgive me."

"I..." I started, choking on my words a little. "I think we can forgive you. But it's going to take time."

"We need you to be there for us," Ivy said, her voice still quiet. "Always."

"I should have been," Father repeated. He squeezed our hands and then let go, sitting back in the chair. "I feel as though I've been walking around with my eyes closed. Suddenly I feel awake, and it's painful, but... I can see now."

It made sense. That was how it had always seemed to me too. Like Father wasn't really there. He was just existing, not really living. I'd just never been able to find the words for it.

We both stayed silent, the thoughts echoing around our heads.

He rubbed his tired eyes. "If there's anything I can do to make a start..."

"We'll let you know," I told him.

Ivy stood up, then, and for a second I wasn't sure what she was going to do. But she walked over to Father's chair and hugged him. After a moment, I joined in.

"I really am sorry," he said quietly. "I don't think I can say it enough."

I blinked back tears, and saw my twin doing the same. Maybe it was too good to be true, but in that moment, I was certain that our father really meant what he was saying.

When we stepped back, I thought of something I needed to ask. "What will you do? Now that Edith is gone?"

Father's face fell a little. "Well, my job has allowed me some sickness leave. I thought I would go and stay with my sister. She hasn't been well lately. We could probably benefit from each other's company."

I smiled. That was a good idea. Aunt Phoebe was lonely and scatterbrained, and both of them would be much better off together.

"Things will change," Father said finally.

And I think I believed him.

Chapter Twenty-nine

IVY

It had been one of the strangest weeks of our lives, but now it was Monday and it was time to return to Rookwood School.

For once, I actually felt bad about leaving Father. At least Edith was finally gone for good. And Father would be staying with Aunt Phoebe, so I didn't have to worry so much about either of them.

As we pulled away from the house, though, I started to feel something else creeping in.

The school. The safe. Henry.

We'd been so distracted with everything at home that I'd almost forgotten about the threat to Rookwood. What were we going to find when we got back there? Would the school even be still standing? What if Henry had found the safe and a way to open it? I didn't think Matron would have let him in to her apartment, but perhaps he'd sent her away as well.

I stared out of the window at the passing countryside, wondering if this would be the final time that we'd ever travel there. Scarlet and Father were quiet too, but it felt like a more contented silence than we'd had for years.

Once again there was a queue of motor cars and buses all the way back to the school gates, everyone inching forward as we waited to get closer to the front doors.

It was a relief to see from a distance that the school looked to be in one piece, and that the front doors were wide open as pupils crowded in. When we finally got near enough, we jumped out of the motor car.

"Will you be all right?" Scarlet asked Father as he handed us our bags.

"I'm sure I'll be fine," said Father a little weakly. "Please call me if you need anything."

"Aunt Phoebe doesn't have a telephone," I reminded him.

He scratched his unshaven face thoughtfully. "I will have to get one installed for her... Call her neighbour, then, or write me a letter. I said I'd be there for you."

I hugged him. "We know you're trying. Thank you." I really meant it. It felt so different already. We'd encountered so many adults who didn't care, or didn't listen, or at worst were actively trying to kill us. Now we had our father back on our side. For once it was hard to say goodbye.

This time we didn't meet any of our friends on the way in. Miss Bowler was there in the entrance hall, shouting at everyone to take their luggage back to their rooms, while the secretary winced at the volume of her voice. I caught a glimpse of Mrs Knight standing near her office – so she *had* returned to school. That was good news.

Scarlet took a look around. "I don't see any of these so-called repairs," she said. I nodded in agreement. Had Henry really bothered to fix anything? There was nothing different about the building as far as I could see.

We pushed upstairs through the sea of girls and began along the corridor towards our room, only to find Matron coming towards us. She looked furious, her face red and puffy, and she was carrying two suitcases.

"Well, I never!" she was saying. "Booted out of my own apartment!"

We halted in front of her. It felt as though someone had poured a bucket of ice over me. *Did that mean...*

"Matron?" Scarlet asked. "What happened?"

Matron dropped the suitcases to the floor with a *thud*.

"*Master Bartholomew* has thrown me out. I've been told to stay in an empty dorm room until further notice," she huffed.

"But why?" I asked, even though I had a horrible feeling that I knew.

She grimaced. "He says he needs to have the place inspected. What could possibly need inspecting in there, I don't know."

I could feel Scarlet clenching her fists beside me. Had he found the safe?

Matron bent down and picked up the bags again. "If you need me, I'll be at the other end of the hall. And not in *my apartment*!" she shouted back the way she came, before continuing.

"This is bad," I said.

"More than bad," Scarlet replied in a hushed voice. "He knows it's there! He must do! Come on, let's dump our stuff in room thirteen and then go and have a look."

Once we'd thrown our bags down, we hastened through the crowds towards Matron's apartment. The door was shut, but Scarlet leant up against it. She pulled back, frowning.

"Could you hear anything?" I asked.

She shrugged. "It's too noisy out here." The corridors were filled with people chatting, doors wide open as they unpacked. "But I thought I heard a sort of banging sound."

Just then, the door she'd been leaning against began to creak and we both jumped back, flattening ourselves against the wall.

It was Henry.

He didn't look quite his usual suave self – his hair was unkempt, and his eyes tired. He slammed the door shut behind him and checked his pocket watch.

I tried not to breathe, hoping he wouldn't notice us watching him.

The inspector suddenly came out as well, and they began speaking in hushed voices.

"...damn thing won't open," Mr Hardwick said, wiping his brow.

"Then you'll find a way to open it," Henry told him. He pointed his finger in the man's face. "We need that will. If this is where it is, then..."

Mr Hardwick shuddered a little. "Sorry, sir. I'll do my best. But I don't understand. If nobody knows about this, then why does it matter? When we tear the place down and build a block of flats, who's going to find it?"

Scarlet gasped, and I froze, but neither of them seemed to have noticed.

Henry frowned, deep furrows crossing his forehead. "Now, you listen here. This dump is all I have left, and I'm not taking any chances! If anyone finds out the truth, even if it's by digging the safe out of the rubble, we get *nothing*, you understand? We're finished." He scratched at his forearm while Mr Hardwick just stared up at him, wide-eyed. "Father told me the old bag had probably hidden the real will somewhere, just to spite him. He was right, as always. I *know* the thing is in there."

Scarlet screwed up her face in disgust. I knew how she felt. *To spite him?* He had stolen everything from Lady Wootton – she had every right to try to stop him. And if Henry thought his father was always right... that was a definite warning sign.

"Very well, sir," Mr Hardwick said, when he seemed quite sure that Henry had stopped ranting. "We'll keep trying." He headed back inside.

Henry balled up his fists and curled against the wall, silently seething. After a few moments, though, he stood up straight and walked away. There was suddenly a swing back in his step as if nothing was wrong.

I turned to my twin once we were certain he had gone. "I can't believe it! He just admitted everything! He *does* know about the will. And he wants to turn the school into flats!"

"I knew it," she said. "I knew he was a twisted snake!" She paused. "On the plus side, they can't get into the safe." I could see a spark in her eye.

"Phew," I breathed. "That's a relief." Then I remembered something. "Thank goodness Ebony took the keys!"

My twin nodded. "Even if he didn't have the third key, we wouldn't want to give him a head start." She looked thoughtful for a moment. "Maybe he was trying to break it? That could be what the banging sound was. Judging by what they said, though, it didn't work. We still have time!"

We raced back to our room, where, to our surprise, we found Ariadne waiting outside our door.

"Scarlet! Ivy! You're here!" she cried, throwing herself at us. Once we'd disentangled ourselves, she stood back. "I was worried your stepmother might have killed you!"

"Ah," I said. "About that..."

We ushered Ariadne inside our room, sat down on our beds and set about trying to explain exactly what had happened at home. Her horrified expression said it all.

"No! *Really?*" she kept asking.

But by the end of the story, she seemed happier. "You mean your stepmother is actually gone for good? That's wonderful news for you, isn't it?"

I looked uncertainly at Scarlet. "I think so? I don't know what it'll mean for Father in the long run. But for now, it seems we have him back. And he finally knows the truth about Edith and how she worked with Miss Fox."

"That's a relief," Ariadne said. "Oh, but I need to tell you—"

Just then, there was a knock on the door. I got up to open it, to find Ebony outside, tapping her black boots on the carpet.

"There you are!" she said, peering in. "I thought I might find you in here."

We chorused our hellos to her. "Did you bring the keys back?" Scarlet asked. "Are they all right?"

"Right here," said Ebony, pulling them from her pocket.

"Phew," I said, suddenly remembering what else we had to update them on. "We saw Henry coming out of Matron's room, and we heard him talking to Mr Hardwick. He definitely *does* know about the will and is trying to destroy it. And he has no intention of rebuilding the school. He wants to turn it into flats!"

Ariadne gasped. "He just admitted it?" Ebony, however, didn't look surprised. It was pretty much what we'd expected.

"He didn't know we were listening. And it gets worse," Scarlet told our friends. "They've found the safe."

"Oh no!" Ariadne paled. "But how?"

Scarlet shrugged. "Probably the same way we did. Oh, and he's thrown Matron out and is making her live down the hall. But the important thing is, he doesn't seem to have any keys – or to have broken into it. I think he's stumped."

We all fell silent for a moment. I prayed that my twin was right.

"But so are we," Ebony pointed out.

"Actually…" Ariadne had raised a finger. We turned to look at her. "That's what I wanted to talk to you about. I think I managed to glean something from those documents. But I'm not precisely sure what it means."

That got our attention. "What was it?" Scarlet asked. I could hear the excitement in her voice. Had Ariadne really found a clue?

"It was quite a task to figure out any of what that curly writing said, honestly," she explained. "But I got Mr Burton to help me at home. He's in charge of our library."

I blinked. I hadn't known that Ariadne had a library, but I could certainly believe it.

"We worked out some of it, which was mostly historical detail that I didn't think was relevant, but this –" she pulled out a note in her own handwriting – "made me think."

Lady Wootton had children three, but
one did die in infancy
For long was this child grieved, their
absence like a missing key

"A missing key?" Scarlet exclaimed.

"It certainly seems like an unusual choice of words," Ebony said.

Ariadne nodded. "That's what we thought. It was written in different ink too. I'm not completely certain that we read it correctly..." She screwed up her face. "For a while I thought it said she had three chickens."

"So I suppose her other children must have died later, or when they were adults," I mused. "Because they never got to inherit Rookwood."

But Scarlet wasn't listening to either of us. She was bubbling over with excitement. "This HAS to be a clue," she said, snatching the paper from Ariadne's hands. "But what does it mean?"

"I asked Mr Burton if he had any ideas," Ariadne said, "and he suggested I try looking in the child's grave..."

I frowned. "I can't say I fancy that!"

"Me neither," said Scarlet, though I noticed that Ebony looked a little disappointed.

"There has to be something else," I added. "I can't imagine Lady Wootton would want anyone to dig up her beloved child's grave."

"Good point," said Ariadne. "I wonder if there's a memorial to the baby anywhere? Or a painting?"

Scarlet nodded. "We should look after lessons. We could

search the church and look around for any paintings of children. I'll tell the others too." She grinned. "Maybe we might just get our hands on that will before Henry does after all!"

I wasn't so sure. "What about the combination, though?"

"It could be hidden with the last key," Ebony suggested.

I frowned. I was still worried. What if we didn't find everything? Time was precious now that Henry had the safe.

My twin clapped her hands together. "Cheer up, Ivy! We have a lead! Things are looking up!"

"You're right," I said, forcing a smile. "It's better than nothing."

And it was. But there was still a chance we might never find the final piece of the puzzle. Henry would get away with knocking down the school – and that meant no more Ariadne, no more Ebony or Rose or any of our other friends. No more ballet, no more Miss Finch. No more of the halls that our mother and her friends had roamed. No more of Rookwood's secrets, ever. It was as if the school was slowly disintegrating and falling into ash before my eyes.

But we had one last shot. And it was time to take it.

Chapter Thirty

SCARLET

All I could think about was looking for the final key.

There was a brief distraction in ballet, at least. Madame Zelda was furious that Henry sending us all home had disrupted her plans for choosing the parts for *Swan Lake*. "There will be a delay," she growled, "that was beyond our control. But the parts will still be chosen at the end of this week, you mark my words..."

Miss Finch said nothing, but there was a little quirk at

the corner of her lips. I think she was a tiny bit amused at how furious Madame Zelda was.

I had to dance my best if I wanted the lead role, but how could I? If we couldn't find the key and the combination, the school would be gone. There would be no *Swan Lake*. That was all that mattered.

I felt preoccupied as I moved around the room. Miss Finch's beautiful piano playing washed over me, but it was as if I wasn't really hearing it. Every time I tried to think – *Legs straight! Toes pointed! Turn your head!* – moments later, my mind was back to thinking about that blasted safe.

At one point I must have been staring off into the distance because Madame Zelda suddenly snapped her fingers in front of my face. "Are you with us, Scarlet?"

"Yes, Miss," I said, but that couldn't have been further from the truth. My mind was racing in the other direction.

"Good," she replied. "We would not wish to insult the genius of Tchaikovsky, would we?"

"No, Miss," I said. But honestly, I was thinking that his genius was useless if it didn't help us find this bloomin' key.

When the afternoon's lessons were finally over and we'd changed out of our ballet clothes, we had some time to spare before dinner. And that meant we had time to search.

I'd tracked down the other Whispers in class and told

them about Henry and what we were looking for. Penny was negative, as usual, but eventually agreed. We were going to look at the numerous paintings that adorned the walls of Rookwood and see if any of them portrayed a child who could have belonged to Lady Wootton. Violet had the idea to search the chapel and the graveyard – but Rose had stable-yard duty, so we sent Violet off with Ebony instead. The two of them seemed strangely to enjoy the idea – but then both of them had always been a little creepy.

The downstairs of the school had the fewest paintings, since it was mostly just classrooms and corridors with walls that were fairly recent additions. Penny and Nadia, of course, volunteered to search this level. Ivy and I took the next floor up, the one with all the dorm rooms, while Ariadne went to search what she could of the top floor.

Once we'd ruled out the pictures on the stairs (which all seemed to be of old people and animals) Ivy and I went to opposite ends of the floor so that we could meet in the middle. I paced along, staring at the walls. I tried to ignore the strange looks I was getting from the other girls who passed me on their way to the dorms.

There were quite a few frames filled with stuffy portraits of people in Victorian clothing and even earlier. One was of a woman holding what looked like a ferret. But not a single one of them was of a child.

I was so busy looking at the paintings that I nearly bumped into Ivy when I got back to the stairs. "Any luck?"

She brushed her hands on her dress. "No," she said, sighing. "There was one of a girl, but I wouldn't have said she was an *infant*. That's what the writing said, isn't it?"

I nodded. *"Died in infancy."*

"Hmm," Ivy said. "I checked it anyway, but all I got was dusty."

I heard footsteps hurrying down from above us. It was Ariadne.

"Nothing!" she exclaimed. "Well, I did find a painting of some chickens."

"It's not chickens," I said firmly. "Definitely children. Come on, let's find the others."

We headed back down to the ground floor. There was no sign of Penny and Nadia in the corridor, so we made our way to the entrance hall. The door was wedged open, so we could see in.

"There they are!" I said, about to break into a run as I spotted them near the front desk – but I skidded to a halt when I realised who they were with.

Henry.

I pushed Ivy and Ariadne back against the wall. "What's he up to?" I whispered.

They tried to peer round me. "He's saying something to them," Ivy said.

"That's not good." If he realised what we were doing, he might get to our lead before we could.

I couldn't make out what he was saying, but Penny and Nadia were nodding and replying to him.

"Oh, they had better not be giving anything away," I said through gritted teeth.

"They wouldn't," said Ivy, though I wasn't so sure. Penny had always been a snake.

But after a little while Henry nodded back at them, flashed his trademark grin and then wandered away, his hands in his pockets.

We rushed in. "What happened?" I cried.

"Sssh," said the secretary, frowning at me over her glasses. I glared at her and gestured for the others to follow me outside.

Once we were out at the front, we could talk. It was an unusually warm day, and the air smelt fresh. The light was fading, but it was still enough to see well by.

"He just came up and asked us what we were doing," Nadia explained. "He said he'd noticed we were looking at paintings."

Ariadne bit her lip. "Uh-oh. Do you think he suspected?"

"I'm not sure," replied Penny with a shrug. "He seemed maybe a little suspicious, but everything he says sounds like it's sugar-coated... *ugh*." She shuddered. "I feel like I need a bath."

"What did you tell him?" I pressed.

Penny glared at me. "Nothing, all right? What do you think we are – idiots?" I stuck my tongue out at her.

"I told him Miss Pepper was making us look at the paintings for art," Nadia said.

I breathed out. "Okay. That's probably fine. As long as he doesn't ask *her*."

Miss Pepper was a bit eccentric anyway, so there was every chance she'd forget and think it actually was an assignment she'd given us. We just had to hope that Henry had really fallen for it.

Just then, I heard fast footsteps crunching up the gravel drive. We turned to see Ebony and Violet running towards us.

"We've found something!" Ebony yelled, beckoning to us.

She didn't have to say it twice. We all broke into a run and followed them towards the chapel.

Rookwood School's chapel had been there from the start of the building's history, when it had been a grand house. Most of the residents had been buried in the small graveyard there, which was always a little tangled and overgrown.

We darted through the worn gravestones, past where the hatch had been that led to the crypt where we'd been trapped (which had now been boarded up and very firmly nailed down). Eventually, we came to the back of the chapel, where there was nothing but a few stones that were so old the words had fallen away, leaving blank slates.

"Where is it?" I asked.

"Look up," Violet pointed.

There was a plaque set into the stone wall. It read:

ISABELLA WOOTTON

DAUGHTER OF LADY ELIZA MARY AND LORD

MARCUS JAMES WOOTTON

BORN 3/1/1850

DEPARTED THIS EARTH AGED ONLY 2 YEARS

BLESSED BE THE BROKEN ANGELS IN THE GARDEN

OF THE LORD

"Gosh," Ariadne sniffed. "That's so sad."

I hadn't really been thinking about that. She was right, of course, it was awful, but I was preoccupied with something else. "There's nowhere to hide a key," I said. "It's just a stone, in a wall."

Ebony sighed. "We know. We tried prodding it, but nothing happened."

"But it's *something*," Ivy said, standing on tiptoe and running her fingers over the stone. "This is the right daughter. Perhaps this will give us a clue."

"Hmm." I thought my twin could have a point. I read the words over and over. "That last line – the wording seems unusual."

"'*Broken angels*'," Ebony read aloud. "I thought so too."

I turned and looked around the graveyard. "Do you think there could be a broken angel somewhere here?"

"I'll start looking," Ivy said, wandering away through the grass.

Ariadne turned to me. "What about the numbers? Do you think they could make up the combination?"

I thought about it. "Good idea! Write them down, and we'll find out."

Most of the stones in the graveyard were very simple – plain grey slabs that stuck up like teeth from the ground. But there were a few statues. I could see a couple from where I was standing: a lamb, and something that might have been a book but had lost its edges over time.

"Over here!" I heard Ivy's voice calling from the other side of the chapel.

We all hurried round to find her crouched over a tiny angel statue. Its wings were both broken at the tips.

Nadia leant over it. "It's just an old statue, though. How is that going to hide anything?"

"What about in there?" Violet suggested. She pointed at a glass jar in front of the gravestone, the kind people use to hold flowers. Whatever flowers it had held were long gone, and the glass was just filled with stones.

Ivy stared at it. "Worth a try," she said. She unscrewed the metal lid and gently tipped out some of the stones. We all held our breath.

And then I thought I saw something. A tiny glint in the stones...

Ivy saw it too. She reached in and pulled out... a key. Just like the other two we had.

"Yes!" we all cheered. Ariadne punched the air.

Ivy held the key up to the light. "Let's hope this is really it. It definitely looks right. I can see the inscription."

I turned to the others with a grin. "I think this might actually be it! We might have all the pieces of the puzzle if our guess on the combination is right!"

Ivy scooped the stones back into the jar and replaced it before climbing to her feet. "There's just one problem," she said.

"What's that?" asked Ariadne.

"Assuming we do have everything right –" she took a deep breath – "how are we going to get into the room again?"

Chapter Thirty-one

IVY

We'd been so focused on finding the final key to Lady Wootton's safe that we hadn't thought about how we were actually going to get into Matron's room again and open it. We knew that Henry had the room in his clutches now – how were we to get inside without him noticing?

As we walked back towards the school with very cautious excitement, we heard the dinner bell ringing.

"Emergency meeting in our room after dinner," Scarlet

said, "and before you say anything, Penny, this time it really *is* an emergency."

We ate hurriedly. I barely noticed what the stew of the day was – although it was pretty difficult to tell if they ever changed it. It was always brown and lumpy and had a strangely distinctive smell that never seemed to leave the dining hall.

After clearing our plates, we headed back to our dorm. It didn't take long for all of the other Whispers to arrive.

"Right," Scarlet began, standing up in front of our window. "We have a big problem. Henry has kicked Matron out of her room, and he or Mr Hardwick could be in there at any time. So how do we gain access?"

Nadia raised her hand. "Can't we just do the same again?"

My twin breathed out sharply through her nose. "Who's volunteering to get in the dumbwaiter? Because I'm certainly not—"

"Those aren't the only problems," I said. "Let's say we manage to come up with a way to distract Henry. What if he's left someone guarding the room?"

Penny screwed up her face. "You're right. That 'inspector' might be lurking in there."

"So we have to distract him and whoever else might be working with him. And then find a way in." Scarlet sighed and sat down heavily on her bed.

There was a long silence as we all stared around the room, hoping to find some sort of inspiration.

But then Rose slowly put her hand in the air.

"Rose?" I asked, knowing she wouldn't speak otherwise.

"The fire bell," she said simply.

There was another pause, and then Scarlet clapped and jumped up. "Rose! You're a genius! That'll get everyone out!"

I began to realise what Rose was suggesting. When Mr Bartholomew had started the fire in the library, the fire bell had been rung and everyone had to go outside. The same thing had happened at the Shady Pines Hotel on our school trip, although that had been a false alarm.

Ariadne's brow was wrinkling with worry. "Are you saying we should set it off? I'm not sure... My father would kill me. He says fire safety is always to be taken seriously! Isn't pulling the alarm just as likely to get us expelled?"

"Not if they don't find out that it was us," said Ebony. "I think I can do it. I'm good at not being seen."

Scarlet nodded. "We'll put you on fire-bell duty, then. This could really work! We wait until Henry goes in the room then, when the bell starts ringing and he runs out—"

"Along with whoever else is in there," I added.

"We grab the door and get inside!" Scarlet punched her fist into her other hand. "And the safe is ours!"

Ariadne didn't look convinced. "They'll notice if we aren't

outside with the others, surely? What if Mrs Knight takes the register?"

I thought about it. "We won't have long, you're right. And we're going to need someone to cover for us." I drummed my fingers on my legs, thinking. "It has to be as soon as possible too. Henry could figure out another way to open the safe at any minute!"

"It's time for a plan," Scarlet said.

After several minutes of Ariadne frantically scribbling and crossing out suggestions, we eventually had our plan. It went something like this:

TOMORROW

1: Penny and Nadia - spy on Henry throughout the day - see if he's around the building and watch where he goes

2: Ebony - set off the fire alarm after he goes into Matron's room

3: Scarlet, Ivy and Ariadne (me!) - get inside the room

4: Open the safe (hopefully...)

5: The others - cover for us or cause a distraction until we can get outside

Scarlet read through it and nodded. "Just make sure you burn this after we're done," she said, handing it back to Ariadne. "No use sneaking around if we are found out immediately."

"Just one more thing," Nadia piped up. "What do we do if we actually manage to open the safe?"

Everyone paused for a moment.

"Hmm," I said. "It depends what we find. Hopefully, we find something that can stop Henry. If we don't, well..."

I didn't know how to finish that sentence. If the safe was empty, we were all out of luck.

I awoke the next day feeling a strange mixture of contentment and fear. We had a plan, and it *could* work. We had the keys, we had a guess as to what the combination could be. Now all we had to do was not get caught.

And pray that the safe wasn't empty.

As we headed to breakfast, I was reassured to spot Henry in the downstairs corridor. He was with his inspector, Mr Hardwick, and appeared to be muttering something to him angrily. He seemed oblivious to the glares he was getting from passing girls. He had overstayed his welcome, that was for certain.

At breakfast, we went over the plan as stealthily as possible.

Ariadne was still panicking. "What if we get expelled?" she said.

"That's always a problem," Scarlet pointed out through a mouthful of porridge. "And we never do. Well, except that one time you did."

Ariadne frowned at her.

"If we don't manage this," I said, "there will be no school left to be expelled *from*."

"True," she replied, taking a deep breath.

We went through lessons as if it were just a normal day, but the plot to open the safe dominated my thoughts. I was almost worried that the teachers would somehow read our minds, or see how nervous I was. I spilt ink across my work in English, and in French I couldn't remember how to translate *Could you please tell me the way to the railway station?* even though Madame Boulanger had written it on the chalkboard at the beginning.

The keys were in my pocket, and even though they were small, I felt as though they were weighing me down.

There was just so much that could go wrong. Being expelled clearly wouldn't matter too much anyway if we couldn't save the school, but I still didn't fancy the idea. Worse was the possibility of being caught by Henry. We didn't know what he was capable of.

We were heading back to our room with Ariadne at the end of lessons when Penny came running up to us, out of breath. *"He's just gone into Matron's room!"*

Scarlet looked at me, wide-eyed. "Did you see anyone else go in?"

Penny shook her head. "No, but I've only just got up here."

"Tell the others!" Scarlet said.

Penny went running. I knew the others would have gone straight to their stations after lessons. I wondered exactly how Ebony was going to ring the fire bell without anyone noticing, but she had certainly proved last term that she was great at being sneaky.

We hurried towards Matron's room and came to a halt at the place where we had a good view of the door.

"Come on, Ebony," Scarlet muttered.

After what seemed like only a few moments, there was a dreadful clanging sound as the fire bell began to ring.

We watched as all the girls who were in their dorms spilt out into the corridor.

"Fire!" someone yelled.

"It's probably a drill!" I heard another girl say, but they clearly weren't taking any chances.

And then Matron's door opened. We flattened ourselves against the wall as Henry peered out.

"Oh Lord," I heard him mutter. He turned and looked back in – presumably to his accomplice. "Come on," he said. "We'd better get out. If the cook has set the damn place on fire, I'll be having words."

He held the door open to let Mr Hardwick out ahead of him, brushed his hands on his suit and then sauntered towards the stairs – as if a raging fire would be a mere inconvenience to him.

"*Go, go!*" Scarlet whispered.

Ariadne was ahead, so she ran forward and stuck her foot in the door just in time before it closed. We darted in past her and she let the door swing shut behind us.

I tried to steady my nerves. Our metaphorical clock was ticking. We had no idea how long it would take before the bell would be found to be a false alarm, or someone noticed that we weren't outside with the others.

"This is *such* a bad idea," Ariadne said as she ran through Matron's sitting room to the bedroom. The sound of the bell still rang in our ears, but it was a little quieter inside the apartment.

"Oh, come on!" Scarlet said. "We're so close!"

Together we lifted the painting of Lady Wootton from the wall and set it down as gently as we could. We were met with the sight of the small white door that covered the safe, and Scarlet pulled it open with a sharp tug.

There was the safe – it had been badly scratched, I could see that. It looked like Henry had been trying to break in with various tools. But it definitely didn't seem that he'd had any luck.

I pulled out the keys and put one in each lock. They fitted perfectly. "All together?"

Scarlet and Ariadne nodded. They each took hold of a key beside me.

Despite the ticking clock (or more accurately, the screaming bell), we had to take a moment to look at each other. It was as if we couldn't believe this was really happening.

I took a deep breath, and we all turned the keys with a collective *click*.

"It worked!" I exclaimed. "Now for the combination."

Ariadne pulled a piece of paper from her pocket, on which she'd written the numbers from the memorial. "So we had three, one, eighteen-fifty and two." She peered at the safe. "I think these dials usually only take three numbers."

"Try 3-1-1 first," Scarlet said.

We waited as Ariadne turned the dial with trembling fingers. The thing whirred as it moved. I listened for another click, but there was nothing. Would we be able to hear it over the bell? I tugged on the door a little to check, but it didn't move.

"No!" Ariadne whispered. "Right. I'm going to try 3-1-18." She moved faster this time, but again there was nothing.

"3-1-50?" I suggested, but she was already working on it.

And nothing happened.

"Drat!" said Ariadne. "Drat, drat, drat!"

"3-1-2!" I said desperately. It was our last hope. The sound of the bell was echoing through my ears.

Ariadne's fingers again moved quickly, and then –

Did I hear correctly? Had there been a click?

Ariadne stood aside, her hand over her mouth in surprise.

Stepping forward, I pulled on the cold metal door and the safe finally swung open to reveal...

My own reflection, staring back at me.

Chapter Thirty-two

SCARLET

"This can't be happening," I said, watching my own lips echo the words in the mirror.

It always gave me a strange feeling to be reflected next to Ivy. We were mirror twins, after all. It was as if there were four of us. And it reminded me of being in the asylum, of reaching for my reflection so many times, and only the last time was it really my twin, come to rescue me.

Now I felt like the twins in the reflection were laughing at us. We'd come so far, only to be met with nothing.

"No," Ariadne breathed. I could almost taste the disappointment.

The mirror took up the whole of the safe. It looked pretty old, in a golden frame, and some of the backing was peeling.

"Just a minute!" Ariadne said. "What's this?"

She gently pushed me out of the way and plucked something from the bottom of the mirror. It was a piece of paper. She unfolded it and held it out in front of us. My head was swimming from the clanging bell, and the shock of what we'd found, but I managed to focus enough to read it. In swirling, old-fashioned handwriting, it read:

Dear Edgar,
If it is you who reads this, may
you take a long hard look in the
mirror.
    Lady Wootton

"She can't be serious!" I exclaimed. "Was this whole thing just a prank on Mr Bartholomew?"

I was ready to give up. Henry was going to take the school, and we had *nothing*. Just some hundred-year-old lady's idea of a joke at the expense of our evil former headmaster. What had she really done with her will? Destroyed it? Hidden it somewhere no one would ever think to look?

"Wait," Ivy said, putting a hand on my arm. "What if...?" She was peering into the safe. Then she threaded her fingers into a gap at the edges of the mirror, and pulled.

The mirror fell forward. Ivy lowered it gently.

The three of us leant in. And we saw... a rolled-up piece of paper, tied with a purple ribbon.

I snatched it from the safe. Wordlessly, I tugged the ribbon and unfurled it.

~ THE LAST WILL AND TESTAMENT
OF LADY ELIZA MARY WOOTTON ~

"*This is it!*" I said. "This is really it!" My hands quivered. I was almost scared I would rip the ancient paper.

Ariadne had already begun speed-reading. The thing was long and wordy, but she was always the best reader.

"Here!" she cried, tapping the paper.

In the event of my death, Rookwood is to pass to one of my children. If none of them should remain, the building is to pass into the possession of Johnsons Bank, who will retain guardianship until a buyer can be found. It should continue to be run as a school.

Under no circumstances is Edgar J. Bartholomew, or any descendant of his, to receive ownership of the school building.

"Is she allowed to say that?" Ariadne asked.

I shook my head. I didn't know, but it was good enough for me. "She was *really* furious with him. She obviously knew what he was like." It seemed to me that he had taken all her power from her, and she had fought back in the only way she could. If only Mr Bartholomew hadn't been one step ahead and forged the will. If only there had been someone to find her original will earlier.

"I think she hoped the mirror would throw him off the scent," Ivy said, peering down at it. "Or maybe she really did just want him to think about what he was doing."

"Or both," I said.

I looked deeper into the safe, behind where the will had lain untouched for so many years. Remarkably, the cold metal was not even dusty.

There was one more thing resting inside: an old Victorian photograph in a wooden frame. I picked it up. The photograph showed an elegant, sharp-faced woman with her children beside her in white smocks. All of their sepia-toned expressions were stuck in the rigid gaze of people who'd had to stand still for a very long time for the photograph to develop.

"We should leave this," I said, putting it back carefully. "I think she meant this to stay here, to remember them by."

Ivy nodded.

"Right, what are we—" I started, but I was interrupted – by silence. That sounds strange to say, but it hit my brain like a brick.

The alarm had stopped.

"Oh no," Ariadne said, going pale.

"Come on, we have to get out of here!" I tipped the mirror back up and slammed the door on the safe, hearing it click as it locked. I pulled out each of the keys and shoved them in my pocket. Ivy hurried to shut the door that covered the safe's hiding place, and then we picked up the painting.

"Hurry, hurry," Ariadne was muttering. Henry could be back at any minute. I prayed he wouldn't realise that the fire alarm had been a distraction.

The portrait was soon back on the wall, though it wasn't completely straight. Lady Wootton's painted face stared down at us in disapproval. There was nothing we could do about it now – at least we had the will, and Henry probably knew about the safe anyway. We had to run.

The three of us dashed out of Matron's room and headed for the stairs. The place was empty, everyone having gone outside during the bell, and our footsteps echoed off the walls as we ran.

Ariadne was clutching Lady Wootton's will in one hand, and frantically trying to hide it in her satchel.

In my head, Henry appeared at every corner. *Surely* he was just about to step out in front of us?

But to my surprise, we actually made it downstairs. "We have to go out the back way!" I realised suddenly. "If we go out of the front doors, everyone will notice!"

The others agreed and we quickly turned to head towards the nearest exit at the back of the school.

"We might be able to sneak round without them seeing!" Ariadne panted as we skidded on the gravel path. I nodded. But what if they were looking for us?

As we raced along the length of the east wing of Rookwood, my mind was racing too. We'd found the will! We'd really done it! But what now? Who could we trust? I prayed that we'd be able to get it to Mrs Knight without Henry noticing. Hopefully she would know what to do.

We rounded the corner, and that was when I heard the unmistakable sound of Miss Bowler in full force.

"SETTING OFF THE FIRE BELL WITHOUT CAUSE IS AN EXPELLABLE OFFENCE!"

I stopped and put my hand out in front of the others. "Uh-oh."

"WHOEVER IS RESPONSIBLE WILL COME FORWARD RIGHT THIS MOMENT! And you will answer to ME!"

I could see the whole school gathered, the front rows cowering from the blast of Miss Bowler's voice. The other teachers stood beside her, wincing at every bellowed word.

"No one?" She raised her arms in the air. "There WILL be a register taken and we WILL find out who is missing!"

We had no other option. We needed to get back in with everyone else, and somehow avoid Miss Bowler noticing.

But then we had a stroke of luck. I saw Nadia standing at the back, at the edge of the huge crowd of girls. She caught my eye and then gave a stealthy wave.

HELP, I mouthed, trying to mime with a series of complicated gestures that we needed to join them without being noticed. Nadia nodded and nudged Penny, who looked over at us. They both started whispering to each other.

In the middle of Miss Bowler's tirade, Nadia put her hand up.

Miss Bowler stopped and glared at her. "Miss Sayani, this had better be important!"

Nadia started moving forward, presumably trying to draw Miss Bowler's eye away from where we needed to get to.

"Miss, I think I might know who was responsible for the fire bell going off." Everyone turned to stare at her.

"Let's go!" Ariadne said, and we all rushed forward on tiptoe.

We were going to make it. We were—

I felt a hand on my shoulder.

"Where do you think you're going?"

It was Henry Bartholomew.

Chapter Thirty-three

IVY

The three of us stood as still as statues. We'd been caught.

"You'll have to admit," Henry said, folding his arms, "that this looks rather suspicious. The three of you sneaking about over here."

Where did he come from? I thought. *He must have been standing in the shadow of the building.*

Ariadne had her arm over her satchel. I silently prayed

he wouldn't think to look in it, that he wouldn't connect the fire alarm with the safe.

We didn't say a word.

Nadia had stopped talking. This was *bad*. Now it looked as though she had been about to accuse us.

"Nothing to say for yourselves, eh?" Henry said. He was clearly trying to keep up his jovial pretence, but there was a nasty expression in his eyes.

"What is going on over there?" Miss Bowler demanded.

Henry put his hands out and waved us forward. "I think I have your culprits here," he called.

We started walking. I looked back at Henry, but he was just standing there, looking rather pleased with himself.

We trudged towards Miss Bowler like we were walking to our deaths. I was preparing for my eardrums to burst any minute.

But Miss Bowler didn't start shouting – instead she just fixed us with a curious expression as we neared her. "Really, girls?"

"No, Miss," Scarlet tried, "it wasn't us..."

I could see Miss Bowler's face starting to turn beetroot. She was preparing to scream at us.

"Mrs Knight!" Ariadne squeaked suddenly.

Mrs Knight looked up from where she'd been standing among the other teachers, rubbing her arms. It was getting dark, and there was a light drizzle and a bit of a chill in the air.

"We have something important!" Ariadne said with her voice lowered, gesturing at her satchel in front of her body so that Henry couldn't see what she was doing. "It's about the school!"

Mrs Knight peered at us over her glasses with suspicion, but I think she must have been able to see the fear in our eyes. She stepped towards us. "Girls, this is very serious—"

"We know," I said, hoping Henry was still not paying attention and merely enjoying his victory. If he thought we were just pulling a petty prank, then we might get away with it. "We really need to show you something, Miss."

I felt the uncomfortable tingle of the whole school's eyes resting on us. It was a strange sensation.

Miss Bowler folded her arms. "This is stuff and nonsense! If you girls are responsible for the fire alarm, you will be punished! It's no good begging for help now! You need to face the consequences, young ladies!"

But to my surprise, Mrs Knight put her hand on Miss Bowler's shoulder. "Eunice, give me a moment with these three," she said. She kept her voice low, but it had a no-nonsense tone that I'd rarely heard her use. At a much louder volume, she spoke again. "Everyone, we will take the register and then go back inside. We've made certain that there really is no danger and the alarm has been stopped. These three will be coming with me." She nodded to us, and then walked back up the front steps.

With a gulp, I began to follow. She'd sounded angry, but was that just for show? Scarlet and Ariadne came along behind me. I turned and looked for Henry, but he was talking to the inspector and paying us little attention. *Phew.*

Miss Bowler did not look happy at having her chance to tell us off taken away. She got straight back to her shouting. "Stop gawping, you lot!" I heard her yell from behind us as I turned back. "Start lining up!"

We made the journey to the headmistress's office in silence. I was dreading what might happen next. We just had to hope that we could persuade her.

"Well, girls," she began as we entered the office and stood in front of her desk. "You had better have a good explanation for this, that's all I can say."

She sat down in her chair and looked up at us expectantly.

"We were only trying to save the school," said Scarlet.

Mrs Knight blinked at her. "What?"

Ariadne stepped forward, pulling Lady Wootton's will from her satchel. "Here, Miss," she said. "You need to read it."

Mrs Knight looked sceptical, but she took the paper from

my friend, slid her glasses down her nose and began to read. Her eyes slowly widened.

"Where did you... Where did you get this?" she asked. "Is it genuine?" I don't think she dared to even hope.

"We've been working on finding this ever since Henry arrived," I explained. I wanted to give some context before we ended up having to confess to setting off the fire bell. "We found out that our mother was secretly trying to expose Mr Bartholomew senior all those years ago after she heard rumours that he didn't really own the school – but she never found anything."

"We researched the school's history," Ariadne said with a hint of pride, "and found out that Lady Wootton was the last owner. She'd left a trail to find this." She pointed at the will. "She clearly suspected that Mr Bartholomew was up to no good, and she was right!"

Mrs Knight just gaped, her eyes flicking between us and the will on her desk.

"It was in a safe. We heard Henry talking about his plans to get inside and destroy the real will. He wants to tear down the school for apartments, and he didn't want anyone to find out that he isn't the real owner! Setting off the fire alarm was our only chance to get him out of the building so that we could open the safe," Scarlet said. I noticed that she had tactfully not specified that we'd broken into Matron's room to find it.

"It certainly... looks authentic," our headmistress said, turning the paper over and over. "And this seal seems official. Can you show me where you got it from?"

I nodded. "The safe is hidden behind Lady Wootton's portrait on the first floor."

"There's a note inside signed by her too," Scarlet pointed out. "Basically taunting Mr Bartholomew."

"Girls –" Mrs Knight spoke quietly – "this is truly astonishing. I think you may well have found precisely what we need to keep Rookwood out of Mr Bartholomew junior's hands. I am both surprised and relieved. But..."

I swallowed and squeezed my hands behind my back. I had been hoping there wouldn't be a *but*.

"I'm not sure that he will back down so easily," she finished.

I looked at the others, and I could see the worry in their eyes. We hadn't quite considered that.

"He'll have to, surely," Scarlet protested. "This is absolute proof that he isn't entitled to the school!"

"It is," Mrs Knight agreed, "as long as we can prove its legitimacy. But we mustn't underestimate him, I fear. If we don't play our cards right here, this could backfire on us."

"Hmm," Ariadne said, shuffling her feet on the carpet. "Do you think he might try to destroy the will?"

Mrs Knight looked thoughtful. "Perhaps. I think we need to be prepared for him to try to get out of this."

Scarlet suddenly brightened. "What if we catch him off guard?"

We all looked at her expectantly. "What do you mean?" I asked.

"Well, look," she said. "He thinks we're going to be punished for setting off the fire bell. If nothing happens, he might start to suspect what we were really up to. But say we *pretend* that we're in trouble—"

"You're presuming that you *aren't* in trouble..." Mrs Knight said, looking at my twin over her glasses. "But continue."

Scarlet carried on, unperturbed. "Then we can ambush him with the evidence that he doesn't own the school. That way, he'll have no time to start plotting."

Our headmistress remained silent for a moment, staring up at her currently bare office walls. I wondered if she was imagining one of her motivational posters.

She took a deep breath. "I will have to make sure the other teachers are on board. And we may need some external advice, perhaps from someone a with knowledge of legal or financial matters."

Now it was my turn to have an idea. There was someone we knew very well who had that knowledge. Who had offered to do anything they could to help us.

"I think I know who to call," I said.

Chapter Thirty-four

SCARLET

Mrs Knight had marched us out of her office and in the direction of our rooms. The last of the girls who had been lined up outside were coming in, and we tried to look sheepish as we passed them.

And, of course, we ran into Henry.

He was leaning against the wall in the foyer, looking pleased with himself as usual. "Aha," he said. "The troublemakers."

Mrs Knight did her best to look stern and pulled it off rather well. "They will be leaving us soon," she said.

I tried very hard not to grin.

"Expulsion, eh?" said Henry, examining his fingernails. "Fitting. We can't have that sort of prank going on in such a wonderful school, can we?"

"Of course not," said Mrs Knight with feigned politeness. "Come on, girls, you need to go straight to your rooms."

Miss Bowler came striding in, and Mrs Knight turned to her.

"Miss Bowler, I think we need to have a staff meeting about this incident. Can you gather everyone for me?"

"Right," Miss Bowler huffed.

We left them and hurried upstairs. I felt like laughing until I couldn't breathe. We'd clearly fooled Henry, and now our plan could be put into action.

We spent the rest of the evening explaining to the other Whispers exactly what had happened. Mrs Knight had put the will somewhere safe, but Ariadne did a dramatic retelling of exactly what we'd found.

"*No!*" exclaimed Nadia. "She taunted Mr Bartholomew?"

I nodded. "From beyond the grave. What a woman."

"I can't believe you nearly got caught," said Penny, tossing her hair haughtily.

"Well, it was *your* job to prevent that!" I snapped.

She stuck her tongue out at me. "We *tried*!"

Ariadne put down her notebook and looked at both of us. "Please, you two! We might well have won! This is no time for bickering!"

I gaped at her, a little surprised at being told off by our best friend. But she was right. If our plan for tomorrow's assembly worked...

"Right," I said, clearing my throat and trying to change the subject. "We need to explain what the plan is. Henry is under the impression that we've been expelled." Then I began telling everyone what would hopefully happen at assembly in the morning.

"That's genius," said Ebony. "Well, it is if it works."

"Positivity!" Ariadne piped up, waving her pencil in the air. I hoped her attitude would somehow rub off on the universe. We needed this to work, or everything would be lost.

Rose leant over and whispered something to Violet, who nodded and then said, "Rose knows someone who could be of assistance too. We'll tell Mrs Knight."

"Every little helps," I told them with a grin.

Maybe we could really do this. I felt a hint of pride as I wondered what our mother would have thought. Would she ever have believed that her children would be the ones to finally to defeat the Bartholomews?

That night, Ivy and I lay in our beds, staring up at the ceiling.

"I just can't believe it," she said.

"Believe what?" I asked.

I looked over at her and saw the whites of her eyes in the dark. "Any of this. I would have done anything to get away from Rookwood when Miss Fox first dragged me here. I wanted to run down the drive and never look back."

I sighed. "I didn't mind it at first. I wanted to come here."

"Well, we know that because you stole my entrance-exam papers," Ivy replied teasingly.

"Yes, right," I grumbled. She was never going to forgive me for that. "But it didn't take long for me to realise how awful this place was. Especially... without you."

Ivy grinned, and I felt a bit embarrassed. But I'd meant it.

"Everything is so different now," she said. Her voice sounded wistful. "It's not that I think Rookwood is the *best* school in the world, but—"

"But it's ours," I finished.

"Yes!" she said. "It's ours."

And she was right, I thought. Rookwood belonged to us,

and to our friends, and the memory of our mother... and all the girls who had been here. It shouldn't have belonged to Miss Fox or Mr Bartholomew, and it shouldn't belong to Henry now. I felt certain about that in my heart.

The school had changed for the better and it could change even more if we could give it the chance. And, well – the same was true for me and my twin.

Ivy yawned. "I just –" I heard her say quietly – "want to see how the story ends."

Somehow we did manage to fall asleep. We couldn't be seen at breakfast, just in case Henry realised that we hadn't actually been expelled. Instead, Ariadne and Ebony managed to sneak us up some Rookwood porridge, though I almost wished they hadn't. It was even colder and lumpier than usual.

Mrs Knight came upstairs to find us later. She knocked on our bedroom door and then peered inside. "Girls," she said, "he's here." She paused, wringing her hands. "Henry is going to speak in assembly."

I got to my feet. "We'll be right down."

Our headmistress looked at both of us and took a deep breath. For a moment I thought she was going to say something else, but it seemed like her nerves were getting the better of her. "All right," she said. "All right." And she turned away, closing the door behind her.

I walked over to our mirror and looked into it for a moment. Ivy came and stood behind me, breathing deeply as she straightened her school tie. For a moment there were four of us, looking into each other's eyes. For some strange reason, it reassured me. It felt right.

I stroked our mother's hairbrush a few times for luck. We were going to need all the luck we could get.

Even with all the situations that we'd got ourselves into in the past few years – the asylum, Miss Fox, Rose's crazy relatives, our stepmother, confronting Miss Fox again... and again – I didn't think I had ever been as nervous in my life as I was when that assembly began.

I'm not even sure I could tell you why. I think, before, I'd always rushed into everything, hadn't hesitated to fight back. Even when we'd had plans, there would be that adrenaline rush of the final confrontation. This seemed so different, somehow. More grown-up, maybe. More complicated. More chance that things might not go the way that we'd planned.

Ivy and I sneaked in at the back and crouched down a little, so that we couldn't be seen easily from the front. I could feel my heart racing. I found myself staring up at the backs of girls' heads, trying to concentrate on the details of their hair so I wouldn't start hyperventilating.

"Come on, come on," I whispered, glancing at the clock. Assembly was due to start any minute. For now, the hall was still noisy with chatter. Teachers gave disappointed looks from the sidelines. Ivy squeezed my hand.

And then Mrs Knight walked in, shortly followed by Henry.

She was holding a piece of paper and a long envelope, and I could see as she passed us that there was only a slight tremor in her hands.

As they reached the front, I sat up a little straighter. I could see them both quite well over the sea of heads once they were actually on the stage.

"Good morning, girls," our headmistress said from behind her lectern, and we chorused a good morning back.

Henry stood beside her, looking calm, as usual. He had his hands in his pockets and an easy expression on his face – an expression that said he expected things to go exactly his way, just as they had done all his life.

Just you wait, I thought.

"Today is an important day for Rookwood," Mrs Knight began. Her voice wavered a little, but she continued. "Today is the day when we must finally hand the school to its rightful owner."

There was a flurry of whispers that were quickly shushed. Henry just nodded to himself.

"I'm afraid that we can no longer continue in the manner that we have been," Mrs Knight went on, "and therefore things will have to change. And unfortunately, there are laws we must abide by. If a will dictates the true owner of the building, we must follow it to the letter. Isn't that true, sir?"

She turned to look at Henry, who looked a little caught off guard, but quickly answered, "Oh yes, yes, of course."

I squeezed Ivy's hand back. I was praying that Mrs Knight had the guts to go through with this.

"For years we have believed the Bartholomew family to be the owners of Rookwood, and since Mr Bartholomew's son arrived, we were told it would pass to him."

Henry gave one of his winning smiles and stepped forward, looking like he was the king about to give a speech.

"But now we have discovered that this is not, in fact, the case."

The winning smile gradually faded. There was dead silence. Every eye in the school was now on Henry. He frowned, turning towards the headmistress.

Mrs Knight took a deep breath and held up the envelope. "I have here the last will and testament of Lady Eliza Mary Wootton, the last Lady of Rookwood, in which she very clearly expresses her wish that the school should stay out of the hands of the Bartholomew family."

Henry's mouth dropped open and his cheeks began to redden. "What in the...?" he started, but Mrs Knight didn't let him interrupt. She merely spoke more loudly.

"Since Lady Wootton died after her children, Rookwood belongs to the bank. This is the real will; the other was a forgery by the late headmaster!"

This was met with uproar. People were shouting over each other. Henry's fists were tightly clenched and he looked as though he were about to explode.

"Let me see that!" he cried, snatching the envelope out of Mrs Knight's hand. My heart jolted in my chest. What if he tore it up? What would we do then?

He pulled out the contents of the envelope and read it, shaking his head the whole time. The shouts died down as people's urge to see what he would do next overcame them.

"This is ridiculous," he snarled at Mrs Knight, brandishing the paper at her. "Ridiculous. *This* is the forgery. You can't do this."

"I think you'll find she can," said a familiar voice.

And that was when our father walked into the hall.

Chapter Thirty-five

IVY

Henry stood still, looking perplexed, as our father strode across the hall towards him. There was another man following him – Rose's family lawyer. Everyone stared as they passed.

Eventually, Henry regained the power of speech. "Who are you?" he asked them both.

"I'm Mortimer Grey," Father told him. "My children go to school here." I craned my neck to get a good view and saw him hand Henry one of his business cards. "And this is Mr Bloodworth, an attorney and family lawyer to another pupil."

Henry's expression turned back into a scowl. "And what do you think you're going to do?"

"We're going to stop you," said Father simply. "There is proof that you do not own this school. It belongs to the bank."

"Proof?" Henry spat. "*Proof?* This old piece of scrap paper isn't proof of anything." And just to drive home his point, he quickly began ripping the will into shreds.

Everyone gasped. There were cries of protest, even from some of the teachers.

Henry brushed off his hands with a self-satisfied smile as the tiny pieces of paper fluttered to the floor like white butterflies.

"It's a good job," said Mrs Knight quietly from the side of the stage, "that was only a copy of the real will."

Mr Bloodworth, a short man with very little hair remaining on his head, tapped his briefcase. "Locked away safe and sound in here, I think you'll find. And I have verified its authenticity."

A huge sigh of relief flowed around the hall.

"We've got him," Scarlet whispered in my ear. I grinned.

But Henry had clearly begun to realise that his tactics weren't working, and that he needed to try something else. He spread his arms out wide. "All right, so you want the school to go to the bank. Fine. I've got money – I can buy it from them!"

I suddenly felt worried and turned to Scarlet and Ariadne for reassurance, but they looked the same as I felt.

"I'll just buy the building right back and knock the damn thing down," he sneered at Father and Mr Bloodworth. "That's what it needs."

"On the contrary," said Mr Bloodworth, all matter-of-fact. "Rookwood must remain a school. And it is against the lady's final wishes for it to be owned by any member of the Bartholomew family."

I breathed out. I'd forgotten that. A commotion ensued as everyone began talking at once.

Henry now looked up at all of us. "Come on, now. This place is an old heap! I've told you, I'll build a better school. What do you say?"

There was a pause, and then someone a way in front of us stood up. I recognised her from behind as Ariadne's shy friend, Dot Campbell. "No," she said simply, her arms quivering.

There was silence.

Then Ariadne jumped up beside us. "No!" she called out.

I began to see the flow of the tide. I grabbed Scarlet and we both stood. "No!"

And one by one, every girl in Rookwood got to her feet and chanted, "No! No! No!"

The noise was deafening. I felt as though we could lift

the roof off the hall. The sound echoed and reverberated. I even saw the teachers begin to join in.

For once, Miss Bowler didn't shout at everyone to shut up. She was just leaning against the wall, arms folded, not doing a thing to stop it. I saw Miss Finch smiling in her chair, Madame Zelda proudly joining in the chorus beside her.

Eventually, the tide slowed and the noise drifted away. Henry's face had gone red, his fists clenched at his side. We all stayed standing, staring at him, wondering if he would try anything else.

Our father was the first to speak. "You seem oddly determined to keep hold of this place, Master Bartholomew. Could it be that you're perhaps not as well off as you say you are?"

Henry's mouth flapped open and shut like a goldfish.

Father stepped closer. "Perhaps you have certain debts that need to be paid? What is it – gambling on the horses? Failures on the stock market?" He spoke as if they were the only people in the room, but he knew well that all of us were listening. "Were you hoping to rinse every penny you could out of these old walls?"

"You don't know me," Henry retorted.

"Oh, I think I do," said Father. "I know your type. You've never had to want for anything in your life. You're reckless with money because you thought you'd get it all back in your inheritance. Well, your inheritance is a sham, Master Bartholomew, and these girls have proved it."

I felt my heart swell with pride. *We'd done it*.

"I'm not going to stand here and listen to this slander for a moment longer," said Henry. He stomped from the stage. Quiet boos and hisses followed him down the length of the hall.

"I suggest you don't go far, Master Bartholomew," Mr Bloodworth called after him. "And you might want to get a good lawyer."

Henry Bartholomew, with one final revolted glance back at all of us, slammed the door in disgust.

Our lives with our father had been far from fun. There had been so many years where we'd felt invisible to him. He'd given us a roof over our heads, but never a home. I didn't know if anything could make up for that. But in that moment, as the entire hall erupted in cheers, and we knew that we'd really saved the school, for good this time – I felt proud of him. Things were looking better than ever.

The teachers didn't even try to calm things down for what seemed like a good half an hour. We hugged our friends, laughed and jumped around. We even had a celebratory dance with the other Whispers.

Father and Mr Bloodworth stayed up on the stage, talking to Mrs Knight. I wondered what they were discussing.

Eventually, Mrs Knight stepped forward. "All right, girls!" she called out. This time everyone listened, wanting to know what she had to say. "It seems," she said, a smile wrapping round her words, "that Rookwood School will remain open."

Everyone cheered again. It was strange to think how much things had changed. I think people would have relished the chance to get away from the school when Miss Fox or Mr Bartholomew were in charge. But everything we'd been through together had solidified friendships throughout the school, and the place was improving. We felt optimistic, and we weren't going to let another Bartholomew take that away from us.

"Now we need to look to the future," Mrs Knight continued. "We need to see if we can make truly owning the school a reality. I will keep you updated." She clapped her hands together. "But for now – assembly dismissed!"

Scarlet and I waited around for Father as everyone else bustled out of the hall, chatting excitedly. He eventually came over to us, where we stood in the aisle.

"Morning, girls," he said. He was looking well – better than I'd ever seen him, in fact. Our stepmother's poison was wearing off in more ways than one.

We both hugged him, much to his surprise. "Gosh," he said quietly. When we stood back, he was smiling in a slightly embarrassed fashion.

"Thank you," I said.

"Ah, it was nothing," he said, shuffling his feet. "This is the least I could do. We still have a way to go yet. Your friend's lawyer –" he motioned towards Mr Bloodworth, who was polishing his briefcase – "has alerted the bank. It seems we will probably need to buy the school back from them."

"Ah," said Scarlet. "That sounds difficult, since Miss Fox stole a lot of their funds."

"Very true," said Father. "We will see what we can do. I might have to offer my services to help with the school's finances as well. It would be much closer to home here, which would be ideal. I can spend more time with you and Phoebe." He rubbed his hands together. "I think I could really spruce this place up, with a bit of work."

My twin suddenly had an expression on her face that suggested she was about to ask an inappropriate question. Before I could stop her, she blurted out, "But why do you care?"

Father looked a little taken aback, but he took the question in his stride. I hoped that meant he understood what he'd done to deserve it. "I said I would try to make things up to you. If this goes any way towards that, then it's worth it, is it not? And..." He paused, his eyes glazing over for a moment. We waited for him to go on. "When you spoke to me on the telephone, and you told me what your mother had written... that was all I needed to know. This meant a lot to her."

I nodded slowly. "I think it would have been her last wish, to expose what Mr Bartholomew had really done to her friend, and how he'd stolen Rookwood."

Scarlet agreed. "She fought for this place to be better, so that no one would have to go through what she went through ever again."

After a few moments of thoughtful silence, Father put his hands on both of our shoulders. "And now you've done it for her. Girls?" We looked up at him. "You've made your mother proud."

Chapter Thirty-six

SCARLET

The next few days involved a lot of boring financial discussions, from what I could tell. But there was exciting news at the end of it.

Father had rented a room in the village in order to stay close by, and he'd come in each morning for meetings with Mrs Knight. Apparently the school was low on funds, but with help from some generous parents (including Ebony's father, who had renewed enthusiasm after the success of his new play) and investors, they could afford to buy the building from the bank – just.

And soon it seemed our father really did work for Rookwood. He was going to be sorting all of the school's finances from now on, and making sure nothing like what had happened with Miss Fox ever happened again.

I'm not going to lie, it was incredibly strange every time I saw him walking through the school. Like suddenly seeing a camel in the middle of the English countryside – he was something that didn't belong in my mental picture of Rookwood. Not long ago I would have hated the idea of him being there, but now that things were so different... it was okay. It was a little more than okay, perhaps. It was almost... nice.

And another thing: it meant that our stepmother really was gone for good! I hadn't worked up the courage to ask Father if he'd reported her to the police or not, but either way I felt sure she was wallowing in her own misery somewhere. And I thought it served her right. If you give out poison, you'll get poison back.

Trying to carry on lessons as normal was difficult for everyone. All anyone wanted to talk about was whether or not the school would really be saved. Even the teachers eventually gave up and joined in the discussion.

At Friday morning assembly, Mrs Knight took the stage.

"I am pleased to announce," she began, "that Rookwood School will remain open!"

There was thunderous applause, the stamping of feet and cheering.

The headmistress continued once we'd finally shut up. "I think we can all agree that Rookwood is changing for the better, and we want that to continue. There will be no more unreasonable punishments, no more prefects... unless we want them. We will decide the fate of our school!"

I looked around to see everyone grinning and whispering to each other. This never would have seemed possible just a few years ago. Pupils dying, being injured, being locked in asylums... all that would hopefully be a thing of the past. So maybe it hadn't been for nothing.

"And thanks to our new financial adviser, Mr Grey, we are hoping that the school budget will increase, so we can carry out some much-needed repairs and improvements."

"We want new showers!" someone shouted from near the front.

"New ice skates!" yelled someone else.

"No more stew!" cried a third voice, and everyone laughed.

"We'll see," replied Mrs Knight with a grin.

There was a real sense of hope in the air. Maybe Rookwood wouldn't be the worst school in the world for much longer. It would always be old and creepy and full of secrets – but then all the best places are.

Mrs Knight talked a bit more, and threw out a variety of

her famous inspirational statements. For once, I was starting to believe them. When she finally finished, she called Madame Zelda up to the stage.

"Thank you," said Madame Zelda. "I too have an announcement. Now that the school is no longer closing, the ballet recital will still take place. We look forward to seeing you all at the performance of *Swan Lake* at the end of the month."

I gave that my loudest cheer. I looked across at Ivy, and saw her smile – a wide mirror of my own. Our dream was no longer over!

That Saturday night we had the first ever non-emergency meeting of the Whispers. In fact, it was quite the opposite. It was a party.

We'd been to Rookwood village and stocked up on all the midnight-feast sweets that our money could buy. Chocolate drops, sugar mice, toffees, liquorice (I hated the stuff, but Ivy rather liked it), mint humbugs, and my favourite – fizzy cola bottles. We'd all be paying for it next time we had to go to the dentist, but for now it was worth it.

"We've earned this celebration," I said with a mouthful of sweets. I picked up a cola bottle and raised it in the air. "To the Whispers in the Walls!"

Everyone scrambled for a cola sweet, knocked theirs against mine and cheered. We didn't even have to worry too much about the noise – Matron had finally got her apartment back, and I knew she'd be sleeping like a log now that she was in her own bed.

"To Rookwood School!" said Ariadne, and everyone cheered again.

"I can't believe I actually enjoy spending time with you lot," said Penny, rolling her eyes.

"The feeling is mutual," I assured her, poking my tongue out. Penny had spent years trying to make our lives a misery, and she certainly hadn't got any less annoying. But she'd proved her worth. If there was hope for her, there was hope for anybody.

Nadia threw a toffee at me. "It's been fun," she teased.

"It's going to be so wonderful," Ariadne said wistfully. "All of us together, having fun, learning new things..." I pretended to stab myself, but she ignored me. "And no more trouble!" Violet and Rose, who were leaning against each other, gave relieved smiles.

"I quite *like* trouble," said Ebony with a glint of her old witchy mischief in her eyes.

"Me too," I admitted. Ivy grinned and poked me in the arm.

"All right." Ariadne laughed. "Maybe just a *bit* of trouble."

Once everyone had finally become exhausted and gone to bed, Ivy and I lay in room thirteen in the dark, listening to the curtains fluttering in the breeze from the draughty window. The night air was fresh and cold.

"I'm never eating sweets again," I groaned. "My tongue feels furry."

Ivy threw a pillow at me. "I told you to stop!"

I threw it straight back with a *thud*. "You're not my boss," I joked.

There were a few moments of comfortable silence. Even the itchy blankets and lumpy mattress (that still had a hole cut out of it) couldn't ruin my mood.

"I suppose we're stuck here now," Ivy said, though I could hear the amusement in her voice.

"Yep," I responded. "We'll be here all the way until final exams, eating endless amounts of stew."

"Well, it's like we always said..." I turned to see her smiling in the dark. "We can do anything as long as we're together."

The days began to roll by. We would bump into Father occasionally, and he would give us little updates on the school and how Aunt Phoebe was getting on. "Will you come to see us in *Swan Lake*?" I asked him.

"I wouldn't miss it for the world," he said. "Now, back to work."

I'd always thought that Father was a bit addicted to

working, but now that he was employed at our school it didn't matter so much. It was nice just to have him close by.

Ballet was always the highlight of our weeks. We danced our hearts out, and I prayed that Miss Finch and Madame Zelda would notice. Now that the school was saved, I wanted a leading role more than anything. It would be the icing on the cake.

The roles were to be put up on the noticeboard one day after school. Ivy and I raced towards the crowd of girls who swarmed round it. Having just pinned the thing up, Miss Finch was leaning against the wall, somewhat trapped by all the commotion.

And there at the top of the page, I read:

Princess Odette, the white swan – Scarlet Grey
Odile, the black swan – Ivy Grey

"IT'S US!" I shrieked, grabbing Ivy and dancing around in circles. "We got parts!"

"Well," said Miss Finch, her eyes twinkling at us, "the two swans are identical, after all. That's why Prince Siegfried is unable to tell them apart."

"Identical," Ivy said, "but very different."

I grinned. That was us.

Chapter Thirty-seven

IVY

The last dance was about to begin.

It was almost time for the third act of *Swan Lake*. I was waiting backstage at Rookwood, adjusting my black swan tutu for the thirtieth time. The skirt was lined with black feathers that shone like an oil slick when the light hit them.

Once again, Aunt Sara had kindly sent us costumes from her dress shop. They were all so beautiful. I couldn't believe how talented she was with fabrics. As I took a deep breath and straightened up, I crossed my fingers that she had been able to make it to the performance.

Scarlet came and stood beside me in her white costume. "It feels strange," she said. "I feel like you should be the white swan. *You're* the good one."

I laughed. "You're good too, Scarlet. And the swan princess has always been your dream role! Miss Finch knew that."

"I suppose this means she's well and truly forgiven me for smashing her piano," Scarlet said.

"Ha!" I replied.

Nerves were tingling throughout my body. This act was my time to shine. And I hadn't exactly had much experience on a stage – especially since Miss Fox had been trying to kill us at our last recital.

A few moments later, Miss Finch appeared in front of us. "Ready?" she asked, stepping forward and pulling aside the red curtain.

"As I'll ever be," I said.

Scarlet squeezed my hand. "I'll see you at our standing ovation," she said.

I took a deep breath, and walked out into the lights.

I danced my heart out. It was the *pas de six*, where the princesses try to attract the prince by dancing (the prince in this case being played by a fifth year named Maria) but he only has eyes for Odile, who is disguised as Odette. I held my breath as the fanfares rang out for each princess to enter. I knew there were hundreds of eyes watching my big performance, but I tried to forget about it. In my mind, I was back in the ballet studio with Scarlet, dancing with our reflections in the light of the gas lamps...

I had one of the hardest parts of the show to pull off. The famous *fouetté* turns – usually thirty-two of them, although admittedly our version was simplified and Madame Zelda expected a lot fewer. I had to keep my leg raised and whip round many times, trying to stay glued to the spot.

The music swelled as I spun and spun. For just a moment, I *was* the black swan. I felt as though I was flying.

And then, almost as soon as it had begun, it was over, and I was slipping back out through the red curtain, breathless.

Ariadne and Scarlet were waiting for me backstage.

"Yay!" said Ariadne, jumping up and down and clapping.

"Was I all right?" I asked nervously.

"You were brilliant," said Scarlet, patting me on the back as she headed to her position at the side of the stage.

I watched as Scarlet danced the death of the white swan, out in the spotlight. I felt so much warmth in my heart. It was a sight that I'd never have thought possible just a few years ago, when I really believed she was gone forever. Even though it was my twin dancing, I felt as though I were dancing with her.

And, of course, she got her standing ovation. And the rest of us did too, as we went out to face the final curtain. I took my twin's hand as we bowed in the blinding bright lights.

Madame Zelda came on to the stage, shortly followed by Miss Finch. "Well," she said, "I think we can all agree that these girls have done a fantastic job and worked very hard." We curtseyed to our teachers as everyone clapped again. I felt my cheeks flush red. "Thank you all for coming, and we hope you will be seeing more from these talented Rookwood pupils very soon!"

Scarlet leant over and whispered in my ear, "I bet all the ballet talent scouts are just waiting to talk to us."

I laughed. "I think the best we can hope for is to see our aunts..."

As we left the stage and people began milling around in the audience, I climbed down and looked about. There were so many welcoming faces – our friends were chatting to each other, and they all looked happy. I saw Nadia's older sister Meena, who had reassured me back when I'd first joined the school, and she gave me a friendly wave.

All the teachers were there too, sitting together. Miss

Bowler looked unusually pleased, and even Madame Lovelace seemed to be awake, for once. I saw Miss Jones the librarian too, sitting with her niece Jing. Miss Jones appeared to be reading a book about ballet – some things didn't change.

I finally spotted Father a few rows back, looking proud (if faintly embarrassed about it). And beside him was...

"Aunt Phoebe!" I pulled my toe shoes off and dashed over to greet her. I was very pleased to find that my wish had come true.

"Hello!" she said, getting to her feet.

"How are you?" I asked. I really hoped she was doing better after her illness. I didn't think she would have coped well on her own. It was a relief to have her back with Father.

Our aunt gave her usual vague smile. "Oh, wonderful, thank you, Scarlet."

For once, I didn't flinch at being called my twin's name. "I'm Ivy," I responded gently.

Father prodded his sister. "She's teasing you," he said to me. "She knows who you are."

For the first time, I noticed that Aunt Phoebe looked a little cheeky. "Perhaps," she said.

Scarlet came over and joined us, and we had a nice reunion.

"You girls will have to come and stay with us in the holidays," Aunt Phoebe said. "You can show me some more of your lovely dancing."

"You liked it?" Scarlet asked.

"Oh, it was quite charming," replied Aunt Phoebe dreamily. "It reminded me of when I was a girl..."

"Can you remember that far back?" Father teased.

I giggled. It was strange to see Father and Aunt Phoebe together, acting like a real brother and sister once again.

Ariadne appeared beside us. "I'm avoiding Daddy," she said. "He'll only tell me ballet is dangerous or something."

"Good plan," I said. She squeezed my arm.

"Hello, girls," came a voice from further up the aisle.

I turned to see Aunt Sara walking towards us, arm in arm with a lady with long red hair whom I didn't recognise. Both were wearing incredibly glamorous gowns, velvet and sparkly.

I hadn't thought things could get any better. "Aunt Sara!"

She hugged us and said hello to Father and Aunt Phoebe, who greeted her warmly. "So wonderful to see you again!" She turned to her friend. "Girls, this is Laure. We met in Paris." She gave Laure a smile that was as sparkly as their dresses.

"*Bonjour*," said Laure, giving us a tiny wave.

"Remember I told you about my sister?" Aunt Sara began. "Well, there was quite a lot more to that story..."

And so we stood and listened, surrounded by our family and friends, as our mother's story was explained. And of course, we had more to add. The story of Sara and Ida now had a final chapter.

And I had an idea.

"So this is the final meeting of the Whispers in the Walls," Scarlet said.

Room thirteen was filled with all of us again, squished on to the beds and carpet.

"Really?" said Ariadne sadly.

"We can start a new club," Nadia suggested, and Ariadne brightened. "One with a new purpose."

"But we have one last thing to do," Scarlet continued. "Ivy?"

I stood up, took a deep breath. "I think... I think everything that has happened needs to be remembered."

"Everything?" Rose asked quietly.

I nodded. "Everything. Right from the start. Scarlet's diary, Miss Fox, the asylum..."

"Our mother," Scarlet continued, "the death of her friend, everything Mr Bartholomew did, the fire in the library..."

"Miss Fox trying to ruin the school," Penny said, "pushing Josie out of a window, feeding us rat poison..." We all shuddered.

"My family..." Rose suggested. Violet squeezed her hand. "The school trip."

"And everything *I* got up to last term," Ebony said.

"Ugh," Ariadne shuddered. "Don't remind me about Muriel Witherspoon. We're glad to be rid of her."

I nodded in agreement. "And not forgetting everything that's happened this term with the Bartholomews and finding out who really owns Rookwood."

"So what's your idea?" Ebony asked.

I bent down and pulled out a box from underneath my bed, and opened it up. "I got the idea from Scarlet, really. I never would have thought of this if it hadn't been for her writing in her diary, letting me know everything that had happened to her." I reached into the box and drew something out: a diary.

There were some *oohs* and *aahs* and a few confused expressions.

"I've borrowed six of these from our father," I said.

Scarlet pointed at the covers. "And I've expertly customised them."

Scratched into the front of each of the books was a column of letters:

SG
IG
AF
EM
VA

RF
NS
PW

"That's us!" Penny exclaimed, forgetting to look bored and unenthusiastic for once.

Scarlet nodded. "Yep. This isn't just my story any more."

Ariadne raised her hand. "I technically have more initials than that."

"We know." Nadia laughed, rolling her eyes. Ariadne stuck her tongue out in response, and I was amused at seeing our best friend do such a thing. She had come such a long way from when I'd first met her.

I felt my confidence in the idea rising as I thought of how much everything had changed. It just seemed right, somehow. I didn't know what our mother would have thought of it all, but I hoped that Father was correct, and that she'd be proud.

I tapped the diary in my hand. "So we write it all down. Everything that's happened."

"Then what?" asked Violet.

I grinned over at my twin – her face smiling back, just like a mirrored reflection.

That was the fun part.

We did it.

We wrote down every story, every secret. Pages and pages filled with ink all in different handwriting. Everything. Together. Until we had books that told the story of Rookwood, from start to finish – and of lost twins who found each other, and then found everyone else.

And of course, we hid them throughout the school. A puzzle for future generations to solve, just like the puzzles that we have solved.

So if you're reading this, then you know the secrets of Rookwood too.

THE END

Acknowledgements

When I first began Scarlet and Ivy's story during a Creative Writing class at university, I never could have imagined that I would one day get to write six whole books of their adventures! I couldn't have done it alone – there are so many people who have helped to make my dream a reality.

Thanks go to:

All the team at HarperCollins Children's Books – including my wonderful editor, Michelle Misra; Samantha Stewart, Lowri Ribbons, Louisa Sheridan and everyone else who has contributed to the success of Scarlet and Ivy. Thank you all for being so understanding and accommodating when it comes to my health conditions. Also to Lizzie Clifford and Lauren Fortune, my editors earlier on in the series who helped so much to shape it into what it would become.

Super agent Jenny Savill, and all at Andrew Nurnberg Associates – thank you for believing in me.

The illustrators of these editions, the great Kate Forrester and Manuel Šumberac, and to designer Elisabetta Barbazza for giving the series its distinctive look.

My overseas editors, illustrators, translators, and everyone who helps bring the books to a wide audience outside the UK. It is an incredible feeling to know that my books can be enjoyed around the world.

My writing support network – the fab folk at r/YAwriters, #UKMGchat, Bath Spa Uni, Bath Kids' Lit Fest and the fabulous MA Writing Group of Wonders.

My friends and family, and Ed. We have exciting times ahead of us!

And, as always, thank *you* for reading. Now this series has come to a close and you know the last secrets of Rookwood, but I will always have more stories to tell...